D0734899

DEE HENDERSON

THE MARRIAGE
Wish

Steeple
Hill®

Published by Steeple Hill Books™

STEEPLE HILL BOOKS

Steeple
Hill®

ISBN 0-7394-4799-8

THE MARRIAGE WISH

Copyright © 1998 by Dee Henderson

Thou hast turned for me my mourning into dancing.

—*Psalms* 30:11

Chapter One

If Trish sat any closer to Brad, she would be in his lap.

Scott Williams watched his friend keep shifting closer to her husband on the couch and Brad keep trying to squeeze closer to the arm of the couch. Trish was doing it deliberately. Scott's parents, sitting at the other end of the long couch, had plenty of room, but Brad hadn't caught on to that fact yet. Scott wanted to laugh. The games newlyweds played.

No, he had to revise that, it wasn't just the newlyweds. His sister, Heather, was sitting in her husband Frank's lap, and they had been married ten years now. Heather was pregnant again and refused to sit down to rest so Frank had solved the problem. Heather didn't seem to mind. She was flirting with her husband, whispering things in his ear when she thought no one was watching. Frank was enjoying it, Scott noted. He suspected they would come up with an excuse not to linger after the party was over.

His birthday party. He was thirty-eight today. Scott looked at the coffee table and was grateful to see there were only two gifts left. He really appreciated his parents' efforts, and he was enjoying the night with his family and friends, but right at this moment he wished he had spent his birthday alone. He felt lonely, and being here just made the problem worse.

He sat in the winged-back chair, his long legs stretched out in front of him, a bowl of cashews at his elbow and his second diet cola beginning to sweat. His parents had cooked out for dinner, barbecued chicken with roasted potatoes and fresh ears of corn. It had been a fun dinner, it always was when all the family was together, but he hated feeling like a third wheel. It had never bothered him before that everyone but him had someone special, but it was bothering him tonight. For the first time in his life he felt envy and it was a disquieting sensation.

He should be married by now. For years his focus had been on building his career, serving in his church, being a loyal friend, being a much loved uncle to his niece and nephew. He had never thought he needed a wife to make his life complete. He had been wrong.

His gaze settled on Amy a couple steps away, holding his next-to-last gift. When he saw her, his face relaxed into the special smile he reserved just for his niece. She wore the dolphin shirt he had brought back from Florida for her. It was her "most favorite" shirt she had told him when he had arrived that night. Heather said she had trouble getting it off long enough to wash it. Scott grinned. He would buy this little lady the moon if she wanted it. She was four, and he adored her. Amy grinned and climbed into his lap. "Uncle Scott, this feels like a book," she told him importantly. He took the package and weighed it in his hands. "I think you're right. Like to help?" He turned the package to let her at the tape. With full concentration, Amy worked at ripping the paper.

"Thank you, Mom." Margaret had bought him a cook-book, this one on breakfast foods. She knew he loved to cook, had seriously considered becoming a professional chef back in his college days. He didn't have company for breakfast very often; he promised himself he'd rectify that problem.

"I think you'll like the muffin recipes," she said with a smile.

Scott added the book to the small stack of gifts on the floor beside his chair.

"Last one," Greg, his nephew, told him as he brought over a two-foot-long package. Greg was eight years old, further evidence of how time slipped by without Scott re-alizing it. Scott could remember the pleasure of holding him as an infant, could remember the way Greg at two and three had always found him at church on Sunday mornings, and Scott would pick him up and carry him and make him feel important.

"Thank you, Greg."

The gift was from his dad. Scott opened the package as Amy held it steady for him. His eyes lit up when he saw what it was. A new fishing rod. "This is great, Dad." The perfect gift for a man with a new boat.

Larry smiled. "You've about worn out the last one I gave you," he said. Scott had to agree. But that fishing pole was lucky. He had caught his biggest bass with that rod. Still, this one was a beauty. It would be a pleasure to break it in.

He had spent the morning out on the water doing what he did every year on his birthday, evaluating his past year and laying out his priorities for the coming year. It had been hard to face the truth. He was thirty-eight, alone, and even his mom no longer asked when he was going to get married and have a family. As good as his life had been to date, he had been wrong to assume he wanted to spend it alone. He wanted what his friends and family had. He wanted marriage and kids.

The cake was brought in from the kitchen and the candles lit. Scott looked around the group that gathered around the table, especially the kids, and he grinned and turned his attention to the candles. He paused to make a wish.

Lord, how did I ever think I could go through my entire life single? I've enjoyed the freedom and the success in my career, but I never intended it to become a permanent arrangement. There isn't someone to go home to tonight, and I'm feeling that sadness. I really miss not having a wife and having that close, intimate friendship I see in these couples around me. I want to change that, Lord. I want to get married. I want to have what the others around me have. I don't want to be alone anymore.

Scott blew out the candles.

It was a cold morning for late August. The darkness was giving way to the dawn, creating an early-morning twilight. Jennifer St. James pushed her hands deeper into the lined pockets of her windbreaker, trying to ward off the chill. The wind coming off the lake was sending shivers up her spine. The peaceful beauty of the deserted beach, however, more than made up for her discomfort. It had been a difficult night.

She walked along the water's edge, kicking up sand and watching the water smooth it back into place.

"Good morning."

Her older brother had drilled safety precautions into her for so long that she reacted by instinct, her feet breaking into the start of a sprint to ensure she wasn't pinned between water and a threat. No sane person was up at this time of morning.

"Easy!" the man walking a few feet over from her exclaimed, "I didn't mean to startle you."

Jennifer let her sprint fade away and came to a stop several feet up the beach, her heart racing. He had said good-morning. That was all. Good-morning. She'd made a fool of herself again. She felt the heat warm her face. Was she cursed to live her entire life starting at every surprise? She had badly overreacted. She rested her hands against her knees, ignoring the hair that blew around her face, trying to still her racing heart. She watched the man warily as he moved toward her. He was a tall man, reminding her somewhat of her brother's build, probably a basketball player with those long legs and upper-body muscle. As he drew nearer she could see dark brown hair, wavy in a way that made her envious, clear piercing blue eyes and strong features; he was probably in his mid thirties. She had never seen him before, he was the type of man she would have remembered. Not that she came to this stretch of beach very often anymore. Her gut clenched. She hadn't been back in precisely three years.

"Are you okay?" He had stopped about five feet away.

She nodded. Why did he have to be out taking a walk this morning of all mornings? The beach was supposed to be deserted at this hour. The last thing she wanted was conversation with a stranger. She looked and felt a mess. Normally she could care less what she looked like, but when it led to being embarrassed, she cared. Her jeans were the most ratty in her closet, and the jacket hid what had once been a paint sweatshirt of Jerry's.

"I didn't mean to frighten you." His voice was deep and full of concern.

"I didn't realize you were there."

"So I found out."

She straightened slowly, pushing her hands off her knees and forcing her legs to take her weight again, fighting the weakness and the light-headed sensation that hallmarked the exhaustion and dwindling adrenaline.

"You're not okay."

She shied away from the concern in his face, in his voice, instinctively took a step back as he took a step forward. "I had a long night. I'll be fine."

She looked down the beach to the distant grove of trees she had arbitrarily been walking toward. Awkwardly, because he was here and her solitude had been broken, Jennifer turned to resume her walk. The weariness was suddenly weighing heavily on her, and her desire to keep walking was fading, but her only choice was to go home, and that was not an option. She shoved her hair back from her face again and twisted the long hair once, in an old habit, to temporarily prevent it from blowing in her eyes.

"Would you mind if I walk with you?"

She was surprised at the question, surprised at the sudden tenseness in his voice, surprised at the rigidness she saw in his stance as if he had momentarily frozen. She couldn't understand the change. His hands had closed into fists at his sides, but as she watched, they opened and relaxed, almost as if he consciously willed them to do so. He had kept his distance after that one step forward and her one step back. She was not a very good judge of character, but she somehow knew he was not going to be a threat to her. She shrugged. It really didn't matter. "No." He fell into step beside her, slowing his pace to match her slow wander.

They walked along the beach in silence, a few feet apart, both with hands tucked in their jackets, the wind blowing their hair. Jennifer's thoughts drifted back to the night before, and she winced as she remembered, began to mentally draw big *X*s through each scene and force herself to deliberately try to discard the memories. It had worked in the past and it would work again. With time. When the memories faded to the point she could discard them. She sighed, haunted. These memories were not going to go away. Not for a very long time. There was a distraction at hand and she chose to ignore her own rule of respecting silence. "What's your name?" she asked, not looking at him, but knowing he was looking at her. He had been watching her since they started walking and it was a disconcerting sensation. Hers were the first words spoken in several minutes, and the sound of her voice was out of place in the quiet dawn.

"Scott Williams," he replied. "Yours?"

"Jennifer St. James."

She realized immediately her mistake. Questions prompted questions. On this particular morning, even a polite social exchange felt like an intrusion. She breathed a silent sigh of relief when he asked that one question and then went silent. She was grateful he was content with his own thoughts, but she wished he would move his gaze away from her.

"I haven't seen you walking on this beach before. Do you live around here?" he asked eventually.

She shook her head.

"My home is up ahead, off the point," he told her. Jennifer thought it must be nice to live on the lake, be able to enjoy this beach whenever the notion struck. It was expensive property. They walked in silence again and Jennifer hoped the next thing said was going to be goodbye.

"What happened last night, Jennifer?"

His voice was low and deep, the emotion carefully

checked. He had stopped walking and was watching her closely, watching her reaction. "What?" Jennifer honestly didn't know how to answer the question.

"You're married. You have a beaut of a black eye. I want to know what happened, so I can decide what I should do," he elaborated patiently, but tensely. There was nothing idle about his body language or his focus on her.

She didn't answer him right away. What was she suppose to say? She already felt horrible. The last thing she wanted was someone treading in an area of her life where she herself was not yet able to cope. "They are not related."

He removed a hand from his jacket pocket and reached out slowly, clearly afraid he would startle her again, to gently touch the swelling that radiated around her right eye and down her cheek, and when he spoke, the emotion was no longer contained. "Jennifer, this is recent."

His touch burned and made her cringe inside over everything she had lost. "I walked into a door," she said flatly.

He frowned. His entire face tightened at her nonanswer and her rejection of his question. "Jennifer..."

He wanted to help and it was the last thing she wanted. "I don't want to talk about it." Her voice was firm, rigid and laden with warning. Scott wanted to protest. She could see that. All the signs where there. The clenched hand, the set jaw, the eyes that refused to yield the question. But something stopped him, and he pushed his hand back into the pocket of his jacket and nodded abruptly before looking away. Jennifer watched, grateful. He was angry and doing his best not to direct it toward her. She had left an awful dilemma for him, but she couldn't release him from it. She did look battered. She was bruised, tired, exhausted and jumpy. But for the life of her she simply couldn't explain the truth. She could barely cope with it herself. She simply couldn't deal with it this morning.

He started walking again, and she followed him. He deliberately shortened his steps so she would once again be walking across from him. They walked along in silence, and Jennifer could see Scott measuring every step she took, measuring the growing exhaustion, the heaviness of the fatigue that made her veer off center time and time again. She could do little about what he saw. She was exhausted and she knew it and she had no reserves left.

They'd gone more than a mile down the beach and were near a private boathouse and pier when he stopped. "This is my home." He said the words, and she heard that he hated saying them. He didn't want to go. He didn't want to leave his questions unanswered. He wanted to help. She read all of those desires as he stood and looked at her. She did her best to look directly back, even if the intensity of his gaze made her want to drop her eyes and look away. "Could I walk with you a while longer? Would you like some company?" he asked, and she could feel the tug to let him do so.

She shook her head. She suddenly realized what a mess she'd created, and the fact that she had no desire to fix it both amused her and made her sad. She smiled, and it was the first genuine smile she had formed in the past seventy-two hours. "No. I'll be just fine, Scott. Thank you for offering."

He didn't want to hear that answer. "You're sure?"

He was pressing her to change her mind, and her sense of fatigue grew all the greater. She needed to be alone now more than ever. There was no room in her life for company and conversation when there were memories demanding her attention.

Jennifer nodded. "Go on. I'm just going to walk for a while longer," she assured him.

He reluctantly did as she asked. Jennifer watched as he walked up the path to his back patio. She turned toward the grove of trees and began to walk again, determined to not return home until her body demanded sleep and the memories were banished. A few minutes later she was frowning, angry with the fact she now suddenly missed the company. No, not company, him. She missed him. The sun was barely up, and she was thinking about a stranger. She would never see him again, but he had entered her life briefly on one of the toughest mornings of her life, and she would probably always remember him because of that one fact.

Jennifer racked the balls, flipping them to solid, stripe, solid, the eight ball in the center, and sent the cue ball rolling to the far end of the table. The college kids at the next table to the right were laughing at rather crude jokes, and the group of six guys at the bar were boisterous and drunk. Jennifer ignored them with the ease of practice. The first two tables to her left were empty, but Randy and William were playing at the third, and she occasionally tuned in to their conversation, a rather fascinating discussion of a drug case that had been in the papers the past couple of days. The two cops were serious players, and she often played one or the other during the course of an evening. Tonight she preferred to play alone. She broke the rack of balls with a vicious stroke—short, explosive, centered.

She had killed Thomas Bradford tonight.

The chapter, written an hour ago, sat in her briefcase, scrawled by hand on a tablet of white paper while she sat at the back corner booth, shelling peanuts and nursing a diet cola.

The only thing she had left was her career and she had just hung it out to dry. Ann was going to kill her; her agent would not appreciate having the golden goose killed. Jennifer smiled tightly without it reaching her eyes and drilled the seven ball into the rail to send it the length of the table and into a corner pocket. He was quite dead, her detective, Thomas Bradford, the bullets having hit him in the middle of the back and ripped through his chest. He was now as dead as her parents, as dead as her husband, as dead as her three-month-old daughter. Dead.

Maybe she should sell the house.

She contemplated the idea as she moved around the table, laying out her next shot with the precision of someone who had learned to see the game as an interesting study in geometry.

"Jen, what happened? Who hit you?!" The jacket dropped onto the stool next to her, the detective's shield flipping visible. Randy and William both looked over at Bob's words and immediately left their game, heading her way. Jennifer looked up at her friend, annoyed, and then looked back at the cue ball and laid her next shot with finesse, nudging the ten ball into the side pocket without disturbing the eight ball. She wasn't surprised to see him. It was midnight, and Bob Volishburg got off at eleven-thirty. He knew her car. This place was on his way home. He would come in to talk with the other guys from the force, maybe play her a game and then see that she got safely home. He had a mission in life to see that she always got home safely. Compliments of her brother, Jennifer was sure.

"I walked into a door," she replied flatly.

The honest answer went over about as well tonight with the three cops as it had done four days earlier with Scott.

"I was wondering if you would come back," Scott said, stopping a few feet away from her so as not to crowd her space and startle her. His voice was calm and steady while inside his reaction was one of elation. She was back. He had been praying and hoping and working toward this day. She was sitting out on the pier behind his house, dangling her feet over the edge, her hands tucked into the same windbreaker she had worn the last time he had seen her.

He had spent ten days trying to track her down. His conscience had given him no rest. He had finally decided she must have an unlisted phone number. He had tried every St. James in the phone books for the surrounding area. He had ended up calling every battered women's shelter in the surrounding county—not that they would tell him anything, but he had had to try. He had been ready to consider calling the police and the local hospitals, she continued to weigh so heavily on his mind. Then, three days ago, he had his first bit of what he knew had to be providential luck.

He had been browsing a local bookstore when he had chanced upon her picture. She was a writer. The author of a mystery series about a detective named Thomas Bradford. Scott had held the book in his hand and looked at the picture and been stunned at the change in her from the picture on the back of the paperback to the woman he had met on the beach. The book was the paperback release of a previous hardback so he figured the picture was about four years old. The difference was painful to see. Her face was gaunt now. The light in her eyes was gone. What had happened to her in the past few years? Calling her publisher had managed to get him the name of her agent, but there his luck had run out. Her agent—Ann something or other—had refused to give him any information about Jennifer. All he'd been able to hope for was that she would deliver a message.

Jennifer turned now on the pier, drew her knees up to drape her arms across them and quietly looked up at him as he stood at the top of the steps to the pier. "Hello, Scott. I understand you have been looking for me." Her voice was dry and her smile slightly amused.

She looked awful. The black eye had faded to an ugly dark bruise that marred her cheek, and the tenseness in her body and in her face reminded him of a rubber band stretched to its limit for a very long time. "I was worried about you," he said simply.

She nodded and looked down to spin her wedding ring for a moment before looking back up. "Don't be. I'm fine."

Fine compared with what? Her black eye was now an ugly bruise, and she looked as brittle as toffee. She had been exhausted the last time he'd seen her, and the past ten days hadn't made much of an improvement. She looked well past worn out. He walked down and sat on the steps to the pier, close, but not so close as to crowd her. The last thing he wanted to do was give her reason to move. "Been taking another walk?"

"Sort of," she replied. She smiled, and it was a real smile. "I haven't gotten very far."

"Which message finally reached you?" he asked, interlacing his fingers and watching her.

"My agent called. Relayed your message. Really, Scott, 'Come stay with me' does raise a few eyebrows among my friends."

She was embarrassed now; he could see the blush. He knew that his message might cause her some embarrassment with her agent, but it was what needed to be said. He was serious. His home had plenty of guest rooms. He would prefer she accept a place with his sister and her husband, but he would make whatever arrangements she considered reasonable. The idea of someone, her husband, hitting her had haunted him. "I wanted to make sure you knew you had a safe place to stay."

She sighed and dropped her hand to rub it along a wooden beam of the pier. "Scott, I walked into a door."

"So you said," he agreed evenly, very aware of the fact she was not looking at him again. She did it when she didn't want him to see the truth in her eyes.

She looked up. She didn't even look offended that he didn't believe her. She did look like she was in pain. She ran her hand through her hair. "Monday night before we met," she said abruptly, "the third anniversary of my husband's death. I got myself royally drunk. Finally went to bed about 3:00 a.m. When I woke up I headed for the bathroom. I was in a bit of a hurry. I ran right into the edge of the bedroom door." She didn't spare herself when it came to telling the story.

She was a widow. A chunk of his gut tightened. "Jen, I'm sorry. You're way too young to be widow." He put together what she had said, what he had seen, and he winced. "You must have had an awful night."

She grimaced. "That's one way to describe it." The memories of that night came rushing back, and she felt the tension radiate up through her shoulders and neck. She wanted so badly to forget that night. She had thought drinking would help her forget, but it hadn't. If anything, it had simply given her one more memory to regret.

She picked up a small twig the wind had blown down onto the pier and twirled it between her fingers. "How did you find out I was a writer?" she asked, changing the subject.

"I found *Dead Before Dawn* at the local bookstore."

"Honey, it's a perfect title. It's short. To the point. An attention grabber."

"Jerry, there isn't a single murder in the whole book."

"Then let's add one. It's a great title. Great titles are hard to come by."

The memories haunted her. Jennifer tossed the twig she

held into the water and watched the waves push it around. Scott's answer surprised her. The paperback was out already? She had lost track of the publishing schedule. "Jerry liked the title," she told Scott.

Scott wasn't sure how to interpret Jennifer's expression, there was distance there and memories of the past. Did she not like to talk about her work? Jerry—was that her husband's name? "It was a very good book," he told her, trying to feel out what she would consider comfortable to talk about.

He thought she was a very good writer. He had bought *Dead Before Dawn* and read it in one evening, not finishing until well after midnight. He had searched bookstores during the past two days until he found all eight of her books. They were now piled on his nightstand in the order she had written them. He was almost done with the first book in her series, the book that introduced Thomas Bradford. Her series was great. The closest comparison he could draw was to Robert Parker's Spenser novels, and he loved those books.

"I'm glad you liked it." She shivered slightly as the breeze picked up.

"Would you like to join me for breakfast?" The question came out before he realized it was going to be asked. He instantly regretted it. Had he learned nothing about her so far? Give her an opportunity to leave and she was going to take it. She had accomplished what she had come here to do—acknowledge his message and set him straight as to what had actually happened. How many times in the past ten days had he told himself he would be careful not to make her shy away from him again?

He felt an enormous sense of relief when he saw her smile. "That depends. Are you a good cook?"

He laughed. "You'll have to decide that for yourself. I like to think I am."

She moved to stand up, and he offered her a hand, feeling delighted when she accepted the offer. Her hand was small and the fingers callused, and she would have a hard time tipping a scale past a hundred pounds. He lifted her easily to her feet. The top of her head came to just above his shoulder, a comfortable height for him, and her long auburn hair was clipped back this morning by a carved gold barrette. Up close, her brown eyes were captivating. He forced himself to release her hand and step away once she was on her feet. He wanted to reach out and touch her cheek, say he was glad to see her bruise beginning to heal. Instead, he shoved his hands into his pockets and gently smiled as he waited for her to precede him.

The back patio door was unlocked, and they entered into a large kitchen, adjacent to a formal dining room. The coffee was brewed, the aroma rich and strong. Scott placed his jacket and hers across one of the six kitchen chairs and held out a chair for her at the glass-topped table.

His kitchen was spotless, a matter of honor with him. He found that cooking relaxed him, so he spent a lot of time here unwinding after a day of work. "Do you have any preferences for what you would like?" he asked, mentally reviewing the contents of the refrigerator. He had been planning homemade muffins, peaches and cereal for his own breakfast this morning, but that was pretty routine. He wanted this breakfast to be special. Maybe eggs Benedict, or fresh blueberry waffles, he could even do a batch of breakfast crepes with fresh strawberries.

"Since breakfast is normally coffee and maybe toast or a bagel, I think I'll let you decide," she replied.

He turned from the open refrigerator to look at her, knowing immediately that what breakfast normally was, was skipped. The last thing this lady needed to be doing was skipping meals. "Breakfast is the most important meal of the day, you should at least try to have something like muffins and fruit," he told her firmly. "How about an omelet?" he offered. He did a great omelet.

"Sure." She spotted the bookcase he had in the kitchen for his cookbooks and got up to study them. "These are all yours?" she asked, surprised.

"Yes." He started pulling items from the refrigerator. Ham. Tomatoes. Green peppers. Cheese.

He watched as she randomly selected one of the cook-books from the bookcase and opened it. "Why are the page corners turned down?" she asked.

"A favorite recipe," he replied. As the eggs cooked and he chopped the ham and tomatoes and green peppers, he reviewed the dishes he liked to cook, pointing out different cookbooks and which recipes were uniquely good in each one. It was a comfortable conversation. He liked to talk about his hobby, and she was more than casually interested. It was a comfortable conversation that continued as they ate. They split a western omelet between them and a half dozen warm, homemade blueberry muffins. It was not until they finished breakfast that the conversation turned back to personal subjects.

"How did Jerry die?" Scott asked quietly as he sat watching her drink her second cup of coffee. He didn't want to ask, but he needed to know.

She looked out the large window and out over the lake. "He'd gone to the gym to play racquetball with my brother when he collapsed. He died of a massive heart attack."

How old would he have been? Thirty? Thirty-five? "It was unexpected," Scott said, stating the obvious.

"Very."

He looked at the wedding ring she wore. He had noticed

it ten days ago, a small heart of diamonds, and it looked like it belonged. "Was there any warning? High blood pressure? A history in his family?"

She shook her head. "No. He had passed a complete physical not more than six months before."

"I'm sorry, Jennifer." It was such an inadequate response. Her life had been torn apart, and all he could convey was words. She would have felt the loss like a knife cutting into her, especially if they had been a close couple. "You loved him a great deal." Scott made the observation, more to himself than her, but she answered him, anyway.

"I still do," she replied calmly.

He heard her answer and was envious that love could be so enduring. Not many couples had that kind of closeness. No wonder the anniversary of his death had been so painful for her.

She set down her cup of coffee and changed the subject abruptly. "I've decided to end the series of books."

Scott didn't know what to think, both of the abrupt change of subject and the statement she had just made. She couldn't be serious. She had been writing the series for almost ten years. She wanted to end it? "Thomas Bradford is going to get killed?"

"Yes."

"Why?"

"Because it's not the same without Jerry."

"You wrote the books with your husband?"

She nodded.

Scott didn't say anything for some time. It wasn't wise to make such dramatic life changes when you were grieving. But the books had to be a continual reminder to her of what she had lost. "You've been writing the series for years. Are you sure, Jennifer?" he finally asked.

"I'm sure. I've known for months it's something I needed to do."

"What are you going to do once the series is finished?" he asked.

"I don't know."

He frowned, not liking one possibility that had come to mind. "You are still going to write, aren't you?"

"It is the only profession I know."

He leaned back in his chair, thinking, studying her. He had never known a writer before, and it was hard to make any sort of intelligent judgment about the decision she had to make. The sadness he saw in her expression made him frown. She needed some help. She needed to recover. She needed someone to ensure she ate. He forced himself not to follow that line of thinking any further.

"Do you know when you start how the book is going to end?" He had always wondered that. He assumed that knowing in advance would be helpful as far as clues and situations were concerned, but on the other hand, knowing the ending would make writing the book less interesting. Like seeing a movie for the second time.

Jennifer couldn't stop the memory from returning—

"Jerry, you can't kill the gardener. He's the man who stole the will to protect Nicole's inheritance. Kill the gardener and the will disappears forever." Jennifer didn't like the twist Jerry had added to the well constructed story. They had spent two months hammering out the details of a tight story plot and Jerry was changing the game plan a hundred pages into the book. They were out in the backyard, Jerry reclining in his hammock watching the 49ers and Rams game on his portable TV, Jennifer having come outside to find him. She dropped into the lawn chair beside him, retrieving the two pillows on the ground to use as a headrest. She was dis-

tracted momentarily as she realized she had missed the start of the game.

"Who said the gardener was dead?" Jerry asked, handing her a diet soda from the cooler beside him.

"Thanks," Jennifer said, accepting the cold drink. She flipped open the dog-eared manuscript. "Page ninety-six, and I quote, 'The bullet entered the man's chest and did not exit. He fell forward into the cold waters of the lake without anyone seeing his departure from among the living.'" She dropped the script on his chest. "That sounds like dead to me."

The 49ers threw a deep pass which was caught inside the twenty. The discussion paused while they both watched the replay.

"Did I ever say the man in the boat was the gardener?"

Jennifer thought about it carefully. "No. The killer assumed the man in the boat was the gardener."

Jerry grinned. "Exactly."

"Okay Jerry, what are you planning?"

"I don't know," he replied seriously.

Jennifer tossed one of the pillows at him. "Why do you always insist on adding wrinkles to our nicely planned books?" she demanded, amused.

Jerry smiled. "I have to keep you guessing somehow, don't I?"

Scott watched as Jennifer struggled to come back from somewhere in the past and answer the question he had asked. It was not the first time he had seen memories cross her eyes, and he wondered what memory had just made her smile. "Every book we wrote had at least one major change in the plot by the time we finished writing the story. We would construct an outline for the book, then take turns writing chapters. Invariably Jerry would create a few extra twists in the story."

Jennifer rested her hands loosely around the coffee mug

and was amazed at how easy it was to talk to Scott about the past. Normally sharing about her life with Jerry brought back the pain, but not today. They were memories of good times, and she had thought they were gone forever.

She had been so embarrassed by her panicked flight, her reluctance to explain exactly how she had gotten the black eye. It had taken over a week to put the incident into the back of her mind, get past the embarrassment, and thankfully accept the fact she would never have to see Scott Williams again. The next morning her agent had called. Jennifer had wanted to crawl into a hole and die. Her one consolation had been the mistaken belief that Scott would have at least let the incident go. It had taken her forty-eight hours to work up the nerve to come back to this beach. She was glad now she had. Glad that now he knew the truth.

"You know what I do for a living, what about you, Scott?"

"I'm CEO of an electronics firm called Johnson Electronics."

"Really?" She had expected him to be high up in some corporate setting, but she had not expected this answer. "How long have you been CEO?"

"Three years. They've been good years for the industry, so I haven't had to weather my first downturn in the business. How well we do then will determine how good I am at this job."

Interesting answer. A man who considered his performance under adversity to be the true measure of this worth. "You've been at Johnson Electronics a long time?" He was young to be a CEO.

"Eighteen years. I started out as a draftsman during my junior college days. I worked as an electrical engineer, got an MBA and moved into management."

Jennifer asked him about every facet of the business she could think of—products, competitors, partners, financial numbers. She found the picture he presented of his company fascinating. He shared the smallest details, and she found his grasp of the business remarkable. It was obvious he loved his job. They talked for another thirty minutes before Jennifer rose to her feet and said it was time for her to be leaving.

"Jennifer, I've got tickets for the musical *Chess* next Saturday night. It's an old play, kind of dated, but it's a benefit performance and will be well attended. Would you like to join me?"

His offer caught her by surprise. She had to think about it for a few moments. She had not been on a date since Jerry died. She'd had no desire to. "Thank you, Scott, I would like that," she finally replied. She was lonely. She knew it. And he was good no-pressure company. A night out would be a welcome diversion.

"The play starts at eight-thirty. I'll pick you up at seven and we can have dinner first?"

She smiled and wondered how far he would extend the invitation if she let him. Dinner before and coffee afterward? "Sure, we can do dinner first," she agreed.

He grinned and she liked the grin. "Good. I want an address and a phone number."

She laughed. "I like my privacy, hence the unlisted phone number." She wrote down the information on a piece of paper he pulled from a notepad beside the phone.

As he walked with her across the back patio and down to the beach, she slipped on her jacket and freed her long hair from the collar. "Thank you for breakfast, Scott."

"It was my pleasure, Jennifer. I'll pick you up at seven o'clock Saturday."

Chapter Two

She was late. Jennifer rushed up the front walk of her home, fumbling with her keys. Scott was going to arrive in less than an hour. Her detour to Rachel and Peter's to drop off a book had been a mistake. Her brother had wanted to debate the wisdom of her ending the Thomas Bradford mystery series and she hadn't been able to invent an adequate excuse to leave. She knew better than to mention Scott and a date. She would never have gotten out of there. Peter took the responsibility of being her older brother very seriously.

Jennifer pushed open the front door to be met with the fragrant smell of roses. The bouquet sitting in the center of her dining room table had arrived Wednesday. Three dozen red, white and peach roses. The card had simply said "Looking forward to Saturday—Scott." Jennifer had started crying. She couldn't help it. It had been a long time since anyone had sent her roses.

"Jerry, I got a special delivery today." Jennifer was curled up beside her husband on the couch, using his shoulder as a pillow. The credits of the late, late movie were beginning to roll by.

"You did?" Jerry asked, feigning surprise. His finger gently traced the curve of her jaw.

She smiled. *"I think it was a bribe."*

"What was it?"

"Two dozen red roses."

"It was a bribe," Jerry agreed. *"You know how much red roses cost these days?"* he asked, amused.

She giggled.

"So what do you suppose this mystery person wants?"

Jerry leaned down to kiss her. *"That's hard to say,"* he said softly. *"I suppose you had better ask him."*

Jennifer turned on the couch to face him. *"So what do you think my husband would like in return for two dozen red roses?"*

The memory stopped Jennifer in the doorway. She sighed. These memories were going to drive her crazy.

She dressed with care. She had shopped for a new outfit. Those in her closet held too many memories. She had found a light green, long-sleeved dress. It looked expensive, moved with grace, and it helped her badly shaking self-esteem. She had bought a purse and new shoes to go with the dress. The gold necklace and earrings she wore had been a gift from Jerry.

She was ready before Scott arrived. To keep from pacing back and forth Jennifer went into her office, picked up the black three-ring binder on her desk and the red pen beside it. She turned on the stereo, already tuned to a favorite jazz station. Finding the page marked with a paper clip, she picked up the work where she'd left off, soon forgetting the time.

The doorbell rang. Quickly slipping the paper clip onto the

top of the page she was on, she set the book back on the desk and went to answer the door.

He stood there, looking at the profusion of flowers growing around her porch, elegantly dressed in black slacks and an ivory dress shirt, contained, comfortable. A pleased smile lit his face as he turned and saw her. "Hello, Jennifer."

She smiled back. "Hello, Scott." She stepped back to let him enter her home. "Thank you for the flowers." She motioned to the arrangement, already nervous.

"You're welcome," Scott replied easily. "Did you have a good week?"

"Quiet," she replied. "Let me get my purse and jacket and I'll be ready to go."

She entered the living room, and he followed her. It was a simple room. A fireplace, couch, coffee table, easy chair, two end tables, display shelves. A prominent bookshelf held all the Thomas Bradford first editions.

The pictures caught Scott's attention. There were several on the fireplace mantel, one on the end table. Her wedding picture. Jerry. Scott looked at the picture for several moments. His competition. He was surprised at the feeling, but it could not be ignored. He was competing with Jennifer's memories of Jerry. Jennifer looked different in the pictures. She looked young. She looked happy. The past few years had taken a great toll.

"I'm ready," she said quietly.

He turned to find she had joined him again. He smiled. "Then let's go."

Scott held her jacket for her to slip on. "You look beautiful tonight," he said softly. The soft green dress had caught his attention the moment she'd opened the door, and he'd been watching it flair around her, wondering at the elegance she presented and how many more surprises she had in store for him. She was beautiful. Her face had healed, and while she still looked thin, there was color in her face and life in her eyes tonight.

She flushed. "Thank you."

He gently slipped her long hair free from the collar of the jacket.

After she locked the front door, Jennifer walked beside Scott to his car, an expensive sports car. He held the passenger door, and Jennifer slipped inside. Her car was comfortable and dependable. This car was pure luxury.

"How does Italian sound?" Scott asked, looking over at her inquiringly.

"I love it," Jennifer replied.

Scott nodded as he started the car. "I know a great place."

Jennifer began to relax. Scott drove well, and she found it was a relief to be able to sit back and let someone else manage the traffic. They shared a comfortable silence, rather than the strained one she had feared.

"I've been looking forward to this evening all week," Scott said, breaking the silence.

Jennifer looked over at him, and a chuckle escaped. "The week was that bad?"

Scott gave a slight smile. "I've had better," he admitted.

He reached down and turned on the radio, his eyes not leaving the road. Jazz. Jennifer grinned. Okay, at least they had music in common. He clicked the volume down low. She studied him as he drove and wondered what had made his week so rough. She would have to ask him later. She liked a great deal the fact he was not threatened by the silence between them. She wasn't one to chatter, and silence gave one time to think.

They arrived at the restaurant he had chosen, and the parking lot was crowded. Jennifer had heard of the place, but had never been here before. Scott found a place to park and clicked off the ignition. "Stay put," he told her with a smile. Jennifer took a deep breath as Scott came around the car to open the door for her. She forced herself to smile. It was not Scott's fault that her stomach was beginning to turn in knots again. This was a date, a real, honest to goodness, date. She had conveniently forgotten that fact. Scott offered her his hand to help her from the car, clicked a button on his key ring and all the car doors locked. He offered her his arm. Somewhat embarrassed, Jennifer accepted. He was picking up her nervousness and his smile was kind.

"Relax," he said gently.

"Sorry, Scott. I hate first dates," she admitted, then wished she hadn't.

They were almost across the parking lot. He squeezed her hand. "I know what you mean. Trouble is, you can't have a second one without it." As they reached the door, Scott's arm moved down to around her waist and Jennifer found the touch both disconcerting and comforting. He kept it there as they were escorted by a smiling maître d' to the table Scott had reserved. The restaurant was elegant, the tables spaced for privacy, the lights slightly subdued. Scott helped her slip off the jacket, held her chair for her. He took a seat across from her. Jennifer forced herself to meet his eyes. She knew she was flushed, her face felt hot. All he did was offer a soft reassuring smile. He handed her a menu. "The veal here is very good. As is the quail."

Jennifer nodded and gratefully dropped her eyes to the cloth-covered book that was the menu. She opened it. No prices.

"Jerry, there are no prices in this menu." Jennifer nearly giggled. *"Do you suppose everything is free?"*

Jerry just smiled and motioned the waiter over. "Could we have two coffees please?" He didn't need one. Jennifer did.

His wife had had too much champagne.

He wasn't annoyed. Far from it. She had been petrified of attending the party their publisher had hosted for several writers introducing new books for the Christmas season. She had gone despite the fear and done a magnificent job. When they left the party shortly after eleven, it was with the knowledge that several nationwide bookstore chains would be prominently displaying their seventh book. Their agent, Ann, had sent a bottle of champagne to their hotel room with her congratulations. Jennifer had drunk three glasses. Jerry, who knew Jennifer had been too nervous before the party to eat, had wisely escorted her to the hotel restaurant. She needed to unwind.

"Jerry, let's not do that again, okay?"

"You did a great job, honey."

"I have a headache."

"Too much champagne."

"Too many people," Jennifer replied. "Did you see the lady with the diamond necklace, the one with six strands?"

"Lisa Monet. Her last four books have been on the bestseller list," Jerry replied calmly.

"She was beautiful."

"She couldn't hold a candle to you."

Jennifer smiled. Her husband meant it. "Thanks."

"Sure, beautiful. Want to go dancing after we eat?"

"Could we? It's awful late."

"This from a lady who thinks three in the morning is a perfect time of day?" Jerry kidded gently.

"Only if Thomas decided he wanted to keep talking."

Jerry smiled.

The coffee arrived.

"Jen, have you decided, or would you like some more

time?" With a start, Jennifer realized Scott was address-
ing her.

"The veal, please," she replied, trying to cover the lapse
of concentration.

He signaled the waiter, gave their order, having chosen
veal for himself. "What were you thinking about?" he asked.

Jennifer blushed. "Jerry and I were at a restaurant much
like this in New York a few years ago. I had forgotten that
memory."

"There's no need to apologize," Scott replied gently.
"What took you to New York?"

"Our seventh book came out about Christmastime. The
publishers held a party for all the authors with new books
coming out. A way to generate some publicity."

"I seem to remember reading that that book was very
popular."

Jennifer nodded. "It sold well." *That's why we decided we
could start thinking about starting a family.* She couldn't prevent the look of pain that fleetingly crossed her face.

The salads arrived before Scott could question that look.

They ate in comfortable silence.

"Tell me a little about your family, Jennifer. Do they live
around here?"

Jennifer set down her crystal water glass. "My parents
died a few years ago in a car crash. I have one brother, older
than me. Peter is married, has three children. Alexander is
nine, Tom is eleven, and Tiffany is twelve."

"You and Jerry never had children?" It was the wrong
question to ask; Scott knew it as soon as he asked the question, but it was too late to take back the words.

"Jerry, can we get a Jenny Lynn crib?"

*Her husband's arms around her waist gave her a gentle
hug. "Sure. Next month as a seven month present?"*

"You'll have the baby room painted by then?"

Jerry smiled. "Right down to the teddy bears around the door," he assured her.

Jennifer gave her husband a hug. "Wonderful. I've been thinking about names some more. What do you think about Colleen for a girl?"

"Colleen St. James. I like it. Have a middle name yet?"

"Not yet."

The raw pain Jennifer felt at the memory tore at her heart. Jerry had not lived long enough to see his daughter born. "No," she finally whispered. "No, we never had children."

Scott could see the pain in her eyes. "Jen, I'm sorry. I didn't think..."

She shook her head and forced a smile. "It's okay. I'm not normally so touchy. What about you? Is your family in the area?"

"My parents live in Burmingham, about forty minutes away. I have one younger sister, Heather. She's married and has two children, is expecting her third."

They talked about family for a while, Jennifer laughing at the stories he told of his and Heather's childhood.

"Would you like some coffee?"

"Please," Jennifer agreed.

"How is the book coming?"

"Not too bad. I've actually been working on it for some time. Another week of writing will finish the first draft."

"You are still planning to end the series?"

"Yes. It's best. The books are not the same without Jerry."

Scott looked at his watch and reluctantly said it was time to leave for the theater. Jennifer would have been content to stay and talk for the evening, miss the play.

Scott escorted her from the restaurant, across the parking lot. When he held the car door for her, she was expecting it. "Thank you," she murmured softly, slipping inside.

They were quiet during the few-minutes' ride to the theater. "Have you ever been here, Jennifer?"

She shook her head.

"The theater has seats that circle the entire stage. The stage is an octagon, different parts of which can be raised and lowered during the play. An orchestra will provide the music."

Jennifer smiled. "I'm going to love this, Scott."

Scott held the door for her. They stepped into a massive lobby. Scott, a hand at the small of Jennifer's back, led her into the crowd, angling them to the left. An usher accepted the tickets from Scott, handing back the seat assignment portion along with two programs. "You are in the fourth row in the blue section."

"Thank you."

The seats fanned out from the stage. Jennifer did not see what markers Scott was using until she realized the floor lights along each section were different colors. They were elegant theater seats of royal blue crushed velvet. Scott helped her slip off her jacket and laid it across the back of her chair. The program Jennifer opened was ten full pages of information about the play, the actors, the director, costumes and scenery.

The lights dimmed and the music swelled.

It was a fast-moving play. She hadn't realized it was based on political intrigue.

The intermission, an hour into the play, caught Jennifer by surprise. Scott had been enjoying the play, but he had also been enjoying watching Jennifer, leaning forward in her seat, being totally captivated by the presentation. "Like it so far?"

She leaned back in her seat with a big smile. "Oh, yes." She gave a soft laugh. "I'm exhausted. Too much intrigue."

He chuckled. "You must get tense writing your books."

"After writing a description of a crime scene, it may take me several hours to unwind."

"Jerry, this was a wonderful idea."

The hotel had a gorgeous indoor pool, softly lit and sur-rounded by tropical plants. They were the only guests taking advantage of it. The warm water was easing knots in her back that Jennifer had been afraid would be there permanently. Jerry gently moved his hand up to rub the back of Jennifer's neck where tense muscles were causing her a splitting head-ache. "I wish you would start taking more breaks, Jennifer. Get up and walk around the house if nothing else. These twelve-hour marathons of yours are deadly."

"Hmm." She leaned forward to give him better access to her shoulders.

"How did you manage to get us reservations on less than an hour's notice?"

"I made reservations three weeks ago."

Jennifer opened one eye. "You did?"

He smiled. "I'm not the one who forgets our anniversary."

She groaned. "Guilty. I will make up for the meat loaf din-ner. I just got tied up with the story."

Jerry smiled. "Don't worry about it. I like your meat loaf." He gently kissed her. His arms folded across her waist, support-ing her.

"We're almost done with this book," Jennifer said drowsily.

"Another week," Jerry agreed. He gently rubbed his hand across her midriff. "How's our baby coming?"

"She likes ice cream and chocolate and hates meat loaf," Jen-nifer replied. "And she hates getting up in the morning."

Jerry chuckled. "Nausea still bad?"

"No." Jennifer gently kissed the side of his neck. "It's hard to believe she's six months old," she said with a sigh.

Jerry stole a kiss. "A perfect six months."

"Scott, excuse me. I'll be right back," Jennifer said, her face pale, hands suddenly trembling. She got quickly to her feet. "The ladies' room is along the way we came in?"

Scott's hand steadied her. "Yes." He had seen the emotions rapidly crossing her face. Whatever memory he'd triggered had been a powerful one. He watched as she hurried toward the door.

The ladies' room was actually three rooms, a lounge with beautiful couches and antiques, a powder room and rest rooms. The rooms were crowded with guests. Jennifer moved directly to the lavatory and wet a paper towel. She avoided looking at herself in the mirror, she knew how pale she must look. She returned to the lounge and found a place to sit down.

The racing thoughts didn't settle. She finally forced herself to take a deep breath and get to her feet. She didn't know how long the intermission was, but it was probably no more than fifteen minutes. She had no idea what she was going to say to Scott.

He was standing across the hall from the ladies' room, waiting for her.

He moved to her side when he saw her.

"Sorry about that," Jennifer said quietly, apologetically.

He studied her face for a moment.

"I brought you a drink. It looks like you could use it," he said finally, handing her one of the glasses he carried.

It looked like liquor. "Scott, I don't drink. Except under extreme duress," she qualified, remembering the anniversary of her husband's death.

"Neither do I, actually. It's iced tea."

She blushed with embarrassment.

"Quit that, Jen. If you hadn't asked, I would have been upset."

Jennifer tilted her head to look at him. He was serious. She was never going to get used to this man. "Thank you."

She took a long drink of the iced tea.

"Are you okay?"

He wanted an honest answer. Jennifer didn't know what to tell him. She looked down at the wedding ring she wore. "I remembered forgetting our wedding anniversary the last year Jerry was alive." She forced back the tears, but her eyes were still shining with the moisture. "There are some memories that still wrench my heart, Scott. It's not fair to you. I'm sorry."

Scott slid his hand gently under her hair around the nape of her neck. His blue eyes held her brown ones. "It's okay, Jen," he said softly. "He was your husband. You don't have to forget him in order to go on with your life."

His hand slid down to grasp hers. "Finish your drink. Intermission is almost over."

Jennifer finished the iced tea. Scott took her glass and returned it to one of the waiters mingling through the crowd. He led them back to their seats.

The lights dimmed.

Scott reached over to calmly catch Jennifer's hand, hold it firmly. She squeezed his hand in reply, not looking over at him.

The final act was very moving. Jennifer was crying before the curtain dropped. Scott slipped her a handkerchief. Jennifer squeezed his hand in thanks.

"That was very good, Scott," Jennifer said when the play ended, drying her eyes. "Sad, but good."

"I'm glad you liked it." He intertwined their fingers. "Want to get a nightcap? Some coffee?"

"My place? I really need a couple of aspirins," she admitted.

"Sure." Scott picked up her jacket and their two programs.

"Scott, I *thought* that was you!" His hand stiffened. Jennifer looked up in surprise to see Scott looking back into the crowd.

"Hello, Mrs. Richards," he said politely as a lady in her late fifties stopped at the end of the row of seats, effectively blocking their exit.

"Wasn't it just a divine play? My Susan does such a great job. She has such a natural talent for the part, don't you think?"

Jennifer choked, remembering that Susan Richards had been one of the actresses. She'd played a waitress Jennifer recalled. A very attractive waitress. Scott squeezed Jennifer's hand in response. "Yes, Netta, Susan is becoming a very good actress," he agreed, easing them forward.

"We are having an informal party to celebrate her success. Please do say you will come."

Jennifer saw a beautiful lady in her early twenties wearing a white dress step up beside the older lady. "Mother, that is not necessary." She offered an apologetic smile. "Hi, Scott."

"Susan." He smiled. "Good job, as always. Congratulations on getting the lead for Towers."

She smiled. "Thanks. Jim told you?"

Scott nodded. "Excuse us, ladies, but we need to be going. Jennifer is not feeling well tonight." Before Jennifer realized what was happening, Scott had maneuvered them out into the lobby.

"Susan looks like a nice young woman."

"She is. She's engaged to one of my hardware designers, or will be once Jim gets the nerve to face Netta."

Jennifer had no trouble putting together the full picture. "Oh."

Scott smiled. "Exactly." He playfully squeezed her hand. "You're pretty good at this."

"Lots of practice," Jennifer replied, amused.

"Scott." It was a male voice calling his name this time.

Scott glanced around. "Jen, can you manage a few more minutes? I would like you to meet someone," he asked, looking at her carefully.

"I'll be fine," she insisted.

Scott, his arm around her waist, took them forward to meet the couple. An older gentleman in his late sixties, holding hands with the lady at his side.

"Scott, thanks for the tickets. We enjoyed the show."

Scott smiled broadly, shaking hands with the gentleman. "My pleasure, Andrew." Scott leaned forward to kiss the cheek of the lady. "You look stunning, Maggie."

She blushed. "Thank you, Scott."

"Andrew, Maggie, I would like you to meet Jennifer St. James." Scott's hand around her waist felt very reassuring. Jennifer smiled at the couple as they all said hello. "Andrew in my executive vice president, Jennifer. He knows the business better than I do."

The older man smiled. "Don't believe everything he says, Jennifer. One of these days I may have to retire just to show him I'm not indispensable."

"The day you do, I may resign," Scott answered with a laugh. "Maggie, how's your granddaughter? Still wrapping grandfather, here, around her little finger?"

The lady beamed. "In a big way." She smiled at Jennifer. "Andrew spent the weekend putting up a swing set. My granddaughter is only six months old, but Andrew wanted us to be prepared. In case we ever have to babysit," Maggie said, looking over with amusement at her husband.

He just grinned. "Scott, would you please tell Maggie you can never be too prepared?"

Scott, his attention caught by an emotion that had flickered across Jennifer's face, feeling her sudden tension, had to force himself back to the conversation. He offered a soft smile to Maggie. "Maggie, I think he's determined to always be prepared. You'll have to humor him I'm afraid."

Lord, what's causing Jennifer this pain? I wanted her to have a relaxing night. I don't know what's wrong. Scott prayed the words silently as he shifted his arm to support more of Jennifer's weight. "I hate to say hi and run, but we need to be going," he said to his friends. "Maggie, it was a pleasure. Andrew." Jennifer softly echoed his goodbyes.

They walked together to the car. Scott looked at her closed expression, could see the tension in her and knew she needed some space. He gave it to her. He turned on the radio, found a station still playing soft jazz. "Are you going to be okay?"

Jennifer finally nodded.

"I'll have you home soon," Scott promised.

It was a thirty-minute drive. When they reached her home, Scott came around to open the passenger door and escort her up the walk. She unlocked the front door, then hesitated. "I need some coffee. Would you like to stay and join me?"

Scott knew she must want this evening to simply end. But she was trying to make amends. He silently nodded. Jennifer gestured him toward the living room. "I'll be back in a minute."

She was gone almost ten minutes. Scott didn't crowd her. He walked around the living room. There was a Bible on the end table. Jennifer's name was inscribed on the leather cover. He frowned briefly. What had Jennifer said? He had asked her over dinner where she attended church. "My husband was a very religious man. I haven't been to church much since he died."

Her home suggested that Christianity had not been just one-sided, at least not at some time in the past. There were Bible verses cross-stitched on the throw pillows, two of the pictures had verses of scripture stenciled in. Who knew where she stood now? Other than the clear fact that she was hurting, he did not have much to go on.

It bothered him to realize she had walked away from the one person who could help her heal. God. She had to have felt anger and shock when her husband died, the agony of why it had been allowed to happen would have naturally cut pretty deep. But after three years, there should not still be this distance from God. Was she simply stuck and didn't know how to return? He was going to have to find a way to fix this.

She came back in, carrying their coffee.

Scott accepted the cup she offered him with a quiet thanks. He watched her warily. He had never seen this expression before, the quiet intensity that said she had made a decision.

"I think you chose the wrong time to get to know me, Scott." She took a seat across from him when he sat down on the couch.

He tensed. He suspected this was heading somewhere he did not like. "Because of the memories?"

"Because I don't want to get involved," she replied. "Not now."

He sighed. "Jennifer, you're going to go through this, no matter how long you wait. The first time you venture out, the same set of circumstances is going to occur."

"The memories are too raw, Scott. I can't handle half a

dozen flashbacks every day to a time when life was perfect. I'll shatter."

Scott winced at the image. "Was it perfect, Jen?" he asked carefully.

"For a time, yes, it was," she whispered.

"Do you want me to leave, Jen? Say goodbye for good?"

She leaned her head back and looked over at him. "I want the past back," she replied. She gave a half smile. "I sound like a spoiled child, wanting what I can't have." She sighed. "Scott, I don't think I can even be a good friend right now. I don't have the energy or the nerve to take a risk again."

"Jen, I can't take away the pain you are going through. But I can give you all the time you need, time without any strings attached."

"I get nasty when I'm hurting," Jennifer warned softly.

"I'll survive," he said firmly. "Just don't hide Jennifer. I can't deal with something I don't know is there."

You don't know about Colleen. You don't know how she died.
She looked at his eyes. He wasn't ready to handle that level of her grief. Not yet. "Okay, Scott."

"Good."

Jennifer kicked off her shoes so she could tuck her feet beneath her.

"Would you like to try a simple dinner out this next week?"
She shook her head.

Scott looked disappointed. Before he could comment, Jennifer nodded toward her office. "I've got to get the first draft finished, or I'm going to lose my nerve to finish the series."

He grimaced. "Work. I have used that excuse more times than I care to admit myself. What about the week after?"

"Any night but Monday," Jennifer replied, giving him cart blanche to set her schedule. Monday nights her brother and his two boys came over to watch the football game.

"How about Thursday?"

"Sounds fine," Jennifer agreed.

Scott nodded. "Thursday it is." He couldn't prevent the yawn. It had nothing to do with the company, it had simply been a very long, heavy week.

"Like a refill?" Jennifer asked, gesturing to his coffee cup.

"Please," Scott replied.

Jennifer filled his cup then sat back down. "What other authors do you like to read?" she asked, then grinned. "Besides me?"

He laughed. They passed a pleasant hour, talking about books, authors they liked, then about movies they had seen. Jennifer happened to glance at her watch. "Scott, it's twelve forty-five."

He nodded. "You are right. I had better get going." He got to his feet. He smiled. "I enjoyed tonight."

"So did I," she admitted.

She turned on the porch light and watched him start his car. He lifted a hand. She waved back, then quietly closed the door.

"You look tired. Late night?"

Scott's sister, Heather, grinned as she asked the question, leaning over the back of the pew to get his attention. Busy cramming for the youth group lesson he had to give in twenty minutes, Scott just grinned and said, "Yes. Now go away, Twiggy. And don't tell Mom." The nickname she had picked up in high school had stuck. Scott ensured it got kept alive. She liked to protest, but he knew she would be hurt if he dropped his pet name for her. She had a green thumb and now owned a greenhouse, making her name even more fitting.

She squeezed his shoulders. "I knew it. Is she pretty?"

Scott stuck his finger on the text he was going to use and leaned his head back to smile at his sister. "She's beautiful," he replied gravely. He hadn't told her much when he had reneged on his offer to take her to see the play so he could take Jennifer instead, and her curiosity had to be killing her. Scott loved it. His grin told her he was holding out deliberately.

She swatted his shoulder. "Come on. Spill the beans. Or I will tell Mom you were on a date last night."

"I took Jennifer out to dinner, we went to the play, and then we sat and talked over coffee at her place. I didn't get home till 1:30 a.m. I had a nice time, and yes, I'll probably see her again. Sufficient?"

She grinned. "Not hardly. But you can tell me the rest over lunch. Frank's taking the kids roller skating. You're buying."

"It's your turn to buy," he protested.

"Then we'll go to Fred's," she replied, knowing how he hated the boring food served there.

Scott sighed. "If you're going to twist my arm like that, I'll buy. Why do I love you so much, anyway?"

"Because I've got two kids you adore so you have to be nice to me," she replied with a grin. "I'll find you after church. I'm on piano today."

"Break a finger."

She smiled, tugged his hair, and left him to finish preparing his lesson.

Chapter Three

The doorbell rang just as Jennifer finished turning the caramel popcorn out onto the wax paper. Setting down the wooden spoon, she went to answer the door.

"Hi, Tom." She held open the door for her nephew.

"Hi, Jen," he replied with a big grin. "Dad bought out almost the entire store." He was carrying a full grocery sack.

Jennifer smiled. "He hasn't changed." She could see the cookies and the bag of chips. "Take them straight to the living room, Tom. On the coffee table."

"Okay."

Peter was coming up the walk, carrying Alexander. Jennifer held the door for him. "Thanks." He stepped inside, carrying his sleeping son. "He fell asleep as soon as we got into the car," Peter said softly.

Jennifer nodded toward her bedroom. "Go ahead and put him down."

Her brother nodded and disappeared down the hall.

The roses. Jennifer hurried after Peter. She had moved the roses Scott had sent into her bedroom. Peter would ask too many questions if he saw them.

Peter didn't bother to turn on the bedroom light, and by chance, the door to the bathroom was open, partially hiding the flowers on the dresser. Jennifer helped slip off Alexander's tennis shoes. Peter pulled a light blanket over him.

"Okay." Peter nodded to the door. "I think he'll be fine."

They left the bedroom. Peter didn't notice the flowers.

"Aunt Jen, what channel is the game on?"

"Seventeen." Jennifer smiled at Tom's worried expression. "We're still early, Tom. It's on after this show," she reassured him. "I've got caramel popcorn made if you would like to help bring it out from the kitchen," she offered.

Tom was on his feet in an instant. "Sure."

Peter pulled out glasses, filled them with ice as Jennifer and Tom put the finishing touches on a huge bowl of caramel popcorn. Peter reached around them to sample the warm, slightly sticky caramel mixture. "Good job, Jen."

She grinned. "Thanks."

"Sticky, though."

Jennifer tossed him two clean towels from the bottom drawer by the stove. "For the living room."

He nodded and wisely got one of them damp. He added them both to the tray he was putting together. "Anything else we need?"

Jennifer added two large spoons to the tray. "That should be it."

As was tradition, Peter and Jennifer sat on the floor, using the couch as a backrest. Tom stretched out in front of the fireplace.

"Did Rachel and Tiffany go for their night out?"

Peter nodded. "They left about six-thirty." He opened the box of cookies and offered Jennifer one. She accepted. "They were going to get ice cream, Tiffany finally decided she wanted one of those two-scoop sundaes, then they were going to the show."

"Tom, how was your day?"

Her nephew had pulled out the sports page of the newspaper and was reading intently. "It was good," Tom replied absentmindedly.

Jennifer looked over at Peter and shared a smile. Tom was a reader. A very intense, careful reader. There was always one in the family. Jennifer had lightened up over the years, but she could also be like Tom, totally absorbed in something.

"Tom." Peter finally got his attention. "It's not polite to ignore your hostess."

"Sorry, Aunt Jen," he apologized.

"Look on page 26, there is an article about the state soccer finals," she said, apologizing as well for interrupting him.

"Really?" Tom turned the next few pages. "Thanks."

The show credits rolled by. Peter reached for the remote and adjusted the sound. Jennifer settled back, propped her knees against the coffee table, a cold glass of diet cola cradled in her hands, got comfortable. It was going to be a great game.

"Nice socks, Jen."

Jennifer admired the bright rainbow of colors on her feet. "I bought them for myself last Tuesday." *Right after I bought a very expensive dress to wear to a play you still don't know I went to see.*

The sports page landed back in the basket with the rest of the paper. "There's Grant," Tom said, excited.

They were playing in San Diego and it was a nice night there, low seventies, no wind. Perfect game conditions.

It was a disappointing first quarter. The announcers explained away the repeated pass run, pass punt as the teams were feeling each other out. That was one way to describe it. Jennifer could think of a few others. If a receiver broke free and clear, the quarterback got sacked. If it was a good pass, the receiver dropped it. Punt returns consistently got stopped within five yards. The snacks started to disappear, but there was little excitement among the threesome watching the game.

Tom disappeared into the kitchen at the end of the quarter in search of some ice cream.

"Like a refill?" Peter gestured to the empty glass she was holding.

Jennifer handed it to him. "Thanks. Let's hope the second quarter is not quite so dead."

Peter smiled. "What is it they say about expectations? Low ones are the only kind that don't lead to disappointment?" He handed back her refilled soda.

"Very true," Jennifer admitted. Her right hand slid up the back of her neck and massaged the tight muscles, lessening the pain building inside her head.

"Here, Jennifer, give me back the glass and turn around." Peter had seen the gesture.

Jennifer handed him the glass and turned toward the fire. Peter gently massaged her shoulders. "You've been working too hard again."

"Hmm." The massage felt great. Peter still needed a little practice before he would be as good as Jerry had been, but he wasn't bad at all. "I completed twenty more pages today," Jennifer said, dropping her head forward so Peter could work on her neck.

"You are still planning to end the series?"

"Yes."

"When was the last time you saw your doctor, Jennifer? These headaches are getting more and more frequent."

"Last month. He said to quit crying so much," Jennifer replied, muffled.

Peter's hand worked along the vertebrae in her neck. "Still having bad nights?" he asked, concerned.

Jennifer nodded. "Not as frequently, but yes, I'm still having bad nights," she admitted. She gingerly rolled her head. "That's much better, Peter. Thanks."

"Sure."

"Aunt Jen, do you have any of those chocolate sprinkles left?"

"Try over the sink, Tom." She looked over at her brother. "How in the world can he eat all that stuff and never get sick?"

"I want to know how he can eat all the stuff and not gain weight," Peter replied. "He's a bottomless pit."

"I'm a what?" Tom had returned.

"A bottomless pit."

Tom grinned. "I'm a growing boy, Dad."

Peter gave him a playful swat. "You won't always have that hollow leg."

A sleepy boy appeared in the doorway. Jennifer saw him first. "Hi, Alexander. Come on in."

"Hi, Aunt Jenny. I fell asleep."

"Come sit beside me," Jennifer offered, hiding a grin. Alexander was so adorable when he was sleepy.

"Hi, champ." Peter gave him a hug, lifted his son over to sit between himself and Jennifer. She gently combed his hair with her fingers.

Alexander looked over the food with interest, starting to wake up. "What have I missed?"

"Nothing," Tom replied, somewhat disgusted with the performance of his favorite team.

Jennifer offered Alexander a cookie.

"Nice socks, Aunt Jen," Alexander said gravely.

"Thank you, Alex," Jennifer replied with a smile. His own socks were blue with lots of little brown footballs. It was tradition between the two of them to give each other socks for Christmas; Alex was almost as opposed to shoes as Jennifer.

The second quarter of the game started. The home team actually put together a decent drive before fumbling on the twenty yard line. The phone rang.

"I'll get it," Peter said, motioning his sister to stay put. "It's probably Rachel. She said she would call when they got home." He got to his feet to get the phone in the kitchen.

He was gone only a few minutes. He came back to lean against the doorjamb. "Jennifer, it's for you. He said his name was Scott?"

Jennifer's eyes closed briefly. "I'll take it in the bedroom," Jennifer replied, knowing that statement only dug her a deeper hole, but needing the privacy. She was going to get grilled as soon as she got off the phone. She shifted Alexander so she could get her legs clear of the coffee table. She passed her brother, choosing not to meet his eyes.

In the bedroom she turned on the lamp on the end table. Took a deep breath. Pulling together her nerve, she picked up the phone. "Hi, Scott."

"I'm sorry, Jennifer. I didn't mean to interrupt."

Jennifer cut him off. "My brother, Peter, and his boys are over. We're just watching the Monday-night football game."

"Who's winning?" She could tell he was relieved.

"The San Diego Chargers. The 49ers can't execute even a simple screen pass tonight. It's awful."

Scott chuckled. "I didn't know you were a football fan."

"Monday-night football is something of a tradition at my place," Jennifer explained.

"I just wanted to call and say hi. I'm just leaving work."

"Problems?"

"Just a lot of paperwork to catch up on," Scott replied. "How's the book coming?"

Jennifer pulled her feet up on the bed to get comfortable. "Good. I wrote twenty pages today."

"You sound tired."

Jennifer smiled. Perceptive man. "I am." She propped the second pillow behind her back.

Scott, at his desk fifteen miles away, quietly tapped his pen against the pad of paper in front of him. He had been doodling her name along the edge of the pad of paper, then finally decided to call her. He swiveled his chair around to look out over the surrounding countryside. The city lights were hazy tonight.

"I've got a favor to ask," he said, having finally made up his mind how to handle the dilemma he found himself in. Having canceled out on taking Twiggy to see the play in order to take Jennifer, he was now on the hook to his sister.

"Name it, Scott."

"My sister, Heather, wants to meet you. Would you be game after dinner next week to stopping by her place for coffee?"

Jennifer's memory for certain things was very good. Scott's comment that Heather was pregnant was still clear in her mind. Could she handle meeting her? Jennifer simply did not know. But to say no would force her to talk about some things she simply was not ready to talk about. She forced a lightness in her voice that she was far from feeling. "That would be fine, Scott."

"We won't stay long." Her hesitancy had not escaped him. "Thanks, Jennifer." He glanced at his watch, realizing he'd keep her on the phone almost twenty minutes. "I had better let you get back to the game."

"Thanks for calling."

He smiled. "I'll talk to you later, Jennifer. Good night."

"Good night." Jennifer set down the phone quietly. It was several minutes more before she got the nerve to venture back to the living room.

Alexander had moved down to stretch out beside his brother.

"The 49ers scored just before the half ended. They are ahead seven to three," Tom informed her, his gaze never leaving the display of stats being shown during the halftime break.

Jennifer smiled. "Great. Let's hope they walk all over the Chargers in the second half." She took her seat again on the floor beside Peter. Peter handed her back her drink.

"Who is he?" Peter asked quietly.

Jennifer knew there was no way to duck the questions. Frankly, it was nice to know Peter was still there to run interference. Even if it was not needed in this case. "A friend. We went out to dinner and a play last Saturday night."

"Who is he?"

"His name is Scott Williams. He runs an electronics company."

"Where did you meet him?"

"On the beach when I was taking a walk." In for a penny, in for a pound. "He fixed me breakfast last time." It was clear she had thrown him a hard curveball. Jennifer reached over to put her hand on his arm. "Relax, Peter. You would like him. He's active in his church, single. He's a nice man. He's read all the Thomas Bradford books now. We're friends."

"You like him a lot?"

Jennifer nodded, surprised with how true the answer was. "Very much."

"Does he know about Jerry and Colleen?"

Jennifer looked away. "He knows about Jerry," she replied.

Peter's hand touched her arm. He offered an apologetic smile. "I'm sorry I'm prying, Jennifer."

"That's okay. I've been kind of ducking telling you about him."

"I notice," Peter replied dryly. "That's why you couldn't stay for dinner Saturday?"

She nodded.

Peter gestured toward the other room. "Did he ask you out again?"

Jennifer chuckled. "We already have a date arranged, brother, dear, that was a hi-how-are-you call."

"It takes half an hour to say hi? You who can't stand talking on the phone?"

Jennifer thumped him with a pillow pulled off the couch. "Yes. Now lay off," she ordered with a grin.

"I can't wait to tell Rachel."

Jennifer groaned. "Don't you dare elaborate, Peter. She already suspects something."

"Have you told Beth yet?"

"Are you kidding? She'd be buying a maid of honor dress within the hour."

"Face it, Jennifer. You're surrounded by serious matchmakers."

"Just don't you join their numbers," Jennifer warned.

Peter laughed. "When do I get to meet him?"

"Never," Jennifer muttered beneath her breath.

"What?"

"I don't know," she replied. The second half of the game began, buying her a reprieve. The 49ers finally won the game but it took them until the final few seconds, a field goal giving them a two-point lead.

Alexander was asleep again. Even Tom was nodding off. The caramel popcorn was three-quarters gone, Jennifer and Peter having both begun to work seriously on it during the fourth quarter of the game. Peter got slowly to his feet as the commentators gave the game wrap-up. Jennifer began packing up the remains of the chips and dip and the snack crackers. If they left it with her she would eat it. While her doctor would definitely like her to gain ten pounds, she didn't think this was what he had in mind. Tom held the sack for her. "Thanks, Tom."

"Alex, it's time to go home, son." Peter gently woke the boy. Alex reluctantly got to his feet. "Who won?"

"The 49ers," Peter replied. Alex could not keep his eyes open. Peter picked him up. "I'll be back in a minute, Jennifer. Let me get this one settled in the car."

Jennifer nodded. "Tom, can you reach the porch light for your father?"

The glasses back on the tray, it took only a couple minutes to put the room back in order. Jennifer carried the tray into the kitchen.

"Thanks for having us, Jennifer."

She smiled at her brother. "Same time next week?"

He smiled. "Deal. I'll get Tom to help me make some homemade ice cream."

Jennifer groaned. "I am so full that doesn't even sound good."

Peter looked at the bowl of caramel popcorn. "We did a pretty good job on that," he agreed. He smiled. "Let me know when you hear from Scott again."

She pushed him toward the door. "Go home, Peter."

The phone rang as she was getting ready for bed.

"What's this I hear about you having a date?"

Jennifer sat down on the bed. "And hello to you too, Rachel."

Rachel laughed. "Sorry. Who is he, Jennifer?"

Jennifer settled back against the headrest, using the pillows to get comfortable. It did feel nice to be able to talk to someone who she knew would adore the entire the story. "Do you want the short story or full tale?"

"Peter is putting the boys to bed. Give me the entire story."

"I was walking on the beach. He said hello. Scared the daylights out of me because I didn't realize he was there. You know how jumpy I am when I'm tired. This was the morning after I'd given myself that great shiner. He jumped to the conclusion that I was a battered wife or something, because he apparently tried to track me down afterward."

"Jennifer, you didn't explain?"

"I didn't think it was any of his business. I had just met the guy." She smiled. "The story gets better."

"He found out I was an author and somehow got in touch with Ann because I got this message from her saying that some guy was trying to get in touch with me. She relayed the message he had left and I about died. His message said 'Come stay with me.'"

"Oh, my."

Jennifer laughed. "I went back to the beach, figuring he probably walked there every morning about the same time. Sure enough, I met him again. After I explained the real circumstances, we ended up having breakfast together, and he invited me out to dinner and a play. I had a good time."

Rachel cut her off. "Hold it, Jennifer, I'm still trying to get beyond you had breakfast with him."

Jennifer chuckled. "I like this guy."

"I can tell. What's he look like?"

"Six foot two. Brown hair. Blue eyes. He's thirty-eight. Athletic. He has very expressive eyes."

"Are you going to see him again?"

"Dinner a week from Thursday," Jennifer replied.

"Well I'm glad you're dating again."

"We are becoming good friends, but that is as far as this will ever go, Rachel. Jerry and Colleen are still too big a part of my life to seriously make room for someone else right now. In a couple of years it will be different. Right now is just bad timing."

"Are you sure Jennifer? He sounds perfect."

Jennifer chuckled. "Nobody is perfect. Not even Jerry," she admitted.

"Peter is telling me to get off the phone."

Jennifer laughed. "I told him not to tell you."

"As if your brother could ever keep a secret," Rachel replied. "Besides, I twisted his arm. He had orders to find out where you were Saturday night. I tried to call and you weren't home."

Jennifer laughed. "Thanks, friend. I'll talk to you later."

"Sweet dreams, Jennifer."

Jennifer leaned over to hang up the phone, still smiling.

Ann really was going to kill her. Jennifer dropped the three-ring binder onto the bed beside her and rolled onto her back, groaning as she rubbed bleary eyes. It was after 2:00 a.m. She had taken the printout of the story to bed with her so she could read the entire story and see what sections still needed work. The story was great, and Thomas Bradford was unmistakably dead. She had to warn Ann what was coming. Her publisher was already projecting that two more books would put the series on the bestseller list, and when that happened, demand for all of the books in the series would shoot through the roof. They were not going to be pleased when they got a book that ended the series.

They might not publish it.

It was a possibility she had to consider. But the books were getting strong sell-through numbers and even now they made a decent amount of money. If her publisher declined their contractual option and turned down the book, Jennifer knew Ann would have no trouble placing the book with another publisher. Money was money.

The ironic thing was, this book was by far the best in the series.

Jerry, why did you have to die? Our ten-year plan would have actually worked. Now, I'm going to be starting all over. I miss you, Jerry.

Chapter Four

⚜

Where was page 325? It was almost seven o'clock in the evening on Friday night. Jennifer had been editing the book since seven that morning. Her eyes burned, her throat hurt, she had been reading the pages aloud, and she was hungry. She was not in the mood to be looking for a missing page. She looked through the next dozen pages in the three-ring binder. Pages 326 on, no page 325. The top of her desk wasn't visible, but she'd been working there earlier in the morning. She lowered the leg rest of the recliner and went to search the desk. The phone rang, startling her, and she cracked her knee against the open desk drawer. Muttering under her breath, rubbing the throbbing bruise, she grabbed the phone. "Hello?" A thick binder threatened to slide off the back of the desk and she lunged for it.

"What's wrong?"

Scott. "I just cracked my knee against the drawer, I've lost page 325, and I think I'm seeing double I've been reading so long," she replied, pulling the binder back toward her and forcing it closed. It went back on the shelf.

"Ouch. Put ice on the bruise, try closing your eyes for a while, and can you reprint the page?"

Jennifer laughed. "The printer is somewhere under a stack of books," Jennifer replied wryly, "but I'm working in that direction. Where are you?"

"Still at the office. Have you eaten yet?"

"No, and I'm starved. I forgot lunch. I was on a roll until page 325 decided to disappear."

"Could I interest you in some Chinese food? We deliver."

"I would love some," Jennifer replied, touched by the offer.

"Good. I'll see you in about half an hour."

Jennifer cleared off the printer and reprinted the missing page, hesitated, knowing she should pick up at least some of the clutter since Scott was coming over, but didn't want to lose the time, either. She finally decided the book was more important. She was deeply involved in a chase scene when the doorbell rang. She marked in red where she was at and went to answer the door. "Where would you like this?" Scott asked with a smile. She smiled back, glad to see him.

"The round table in the office," she replied, pointing the way.

"It's getting cold out there," Scott remarked as he entered the office. He set down the two sacks on the table and looked around the room with interest. It was a large room. The walls were lined with bookshelves, the desk had a recent-model computer, and there were work tables at the end of the room spread with documents, newspapers, magazines and file folders. It was a comfortable room, a plush long couch and deep recliner, an open view of the large backyard.

The binders on the shelf by her desk were three inches thick, and he recognized the handwritten names of each of her books across the spines, and there were even a few titles he didn't recognize. Future books?

Jennifer picked up her empty glass. "What can I get you to drink, Scott? I've got coffee made, or there is soda."

"Anything diet is fine."

Jennifer went through the house to the kitchen, refilled her glass from the open two liter of diet soda, found a glass for Scott.

"Where can I find forks, spoons and plates?" Scott asked, joining her.

"The top drawer by the stove is silverware. Directly above that is plates."

Jennifer carried both drinks, leading the way back to the office. "What did you bring?"

He began pulling containers out of the bags. "Sweet and sour pork. Fried rice. Hunan beef. Cashew chicken. You can take your pick or sample them all."

"Everything sounds wonderful." She carefully opened the container of rice. Scott handed her one of the spoons. "Thanks." They both filled their plates. "I didn't realize how hungry I was," Jennifer commented, sampling the Hunan beef.

"I had a meeting over lunch, ended up talking so much I didn't get a chance to eat," Scott admitted.

Jennifer pushed the soft sided package toward him. "Try a wonton. They are delicious."

When the edge of her hunger had been blunted, Jennifer leaned back in her chair. "I could get very used to this."

Scott smiled. "It sure beats eating alone."

"What kept you at work tonight?"

"Shipment problems. Anything that brings down a production line, Peter usually brings me in to settle. Logic Partners has been a good customer for several years. They plan well, let us know far in advance if they are considering a large order. It's a big deal with them if they ever get into a position they have to ask for a fast turnaround of a part. The order we got today asked for a lead time to be reduced by ten weeks. And we had no notion that it was coming. Somebody didn't do their job. Peter thinks the sales manager for the account didn't follow up on some calls as he should have. It's going to be a mess to sort out."

"Not a good day."

He leaned back in the chair. "Today was a sinker, low and away, thrown in from left field."

Jennifer chuckled. "Find some music and take the couch, Scott. Relax." She picked up her drink, then moved back to the recliner.

"Sounds wonderful." He got up to turn on the stereo.

"If you search, you might find the Chicago Bulls game on. They are playing the Pistons tonight," Jennifer offered.

"And you are not listening to it?" Scott teased.

Jennifer held up her hand. "I'm football only. I can follow a baseball game on the radio, but basketball has forever eluded me."

Scott chuckled. He found her preset station playing jazz.

"Nice," Jennifer commented, already back at work.

Scott went to refill his soda. When he returned, he moved the four books from the couch to the floor and stretched out. "I needed this."

Jennifer smiled. "Are you implying you are tired?"

Scott already had his eyes closed. "*Exhausted* describes it better."

Jennifer smiled as she marked out another word. She was listening to the book as she read, fine-tuning the words, just as a master violinist would fine-tune the pitch of his instrument. She worked in silence for forty minutes, adding page after page to the edited pile. She chewed absentmindedly on the plastic cap of her pen as she reached a difficult section. "Scott, is the book on tropical islands over there?" She knew he was still awake, he had just shifted the two throw pillows.

He looked through the stack of books by the sofa. "Here it is." He slid it across the carpet to her.

"Thanks," she answered, her attention never totally shifting from the story. She found the page in the reference book she had paper clipped earlier that day. She frowned. She had got another fact wrong. Jennifer changed the description in the story. How many mistakes in this book had she missed? It was not a pleasant thought.

"What's the matter?"

"I'm rereading the chapters I've written so far. I've got some serious discrepancies. I need to take a class in geography," Jennifer replied abruptly, having just caught another error. Groaning, she got to her feet and crossed to her desk. She pulled up the entire manuscript and did a search for the word *island*. Thirty references. She rubbed the back of her neck where a tenseness was beginning to form. "This I did not need." With a sigh, she printed the list of pages she would have to check.

"Can I help?"

"Yes." Jennifer did not question the offer. She took the list, retrieved the three-ring binder and quickly pulled out the specific pages. "Find where I describe the island and make sure I got the basic geography right. Mount Montgomery has now been both north and south of the capital city. Here," she handed him her red pen, "you are going to need this."

Scott nodded. He watched her pace back to the chair, retrieve her glass. "I'll be right back."

She was annoyed with herself. Scott nearly chuckled as he watched her leave the room, but caught himself in time. It would seem all artists had that temperamental streak; his hardware designers acted the same way.

Jennifer returned in a few minutes to plop back in the easy chair. She picked up the binder, but thinking better of it, dropped it back on the floor. She was getting thoroughly fed up with this book. Too keyed up to sit, Jennifer got up, picked up the books beside her chair and started placing them back on the shelves with the rest of the reference books she had used during the day.

"Only three places need changing," Scott said several minutes later.

"That's all?" She turned to look at him, clearly relieved.

He smiled. "The top three pages."

Jennifer took the pile. She slipped paper clips on the pages, then opened the binder to file them.

"I like what I read, Jennifer." Scott didn't know what kind of comment would be acceptable. Jennifer and her writing was a difficult combination to figure out.

She dropped the binder in his lap. "A book doesn't mean much unless you start on page one."

Scott looked at the binder, back at Jennifer. Was she serious? He knew instinctively that not many people had this privilege.

She shrugged. "I'm beat. That means I'm through for the night. But if you read it, it's on the condition that no comments are allowed," she warned.

He smiled. "Even if I like it?"

"Not even if you like it. I might cut your favorite scene tomorrow because I don't like it," she replied with a smile.

"Okay." Scott settled back on the couch and opened the binder. Jennifer disappeared into the living room to return with her sewing basket. She was making a rose square quilt for Rachel's Christmas present.

Jennifer watched Scott slowly turn the pages of the book, trying to read from his expression what he was thinking. It was impossible. She concentrated on her embroidery.

Half an hour passed. Jennifer tied off the rose-colored embroidery thread. She stuck the fine needle into the pin cushion attached to the top of the sewing basket and sorted through the basket for the light forest green embroidery thread. The end of the thread was frayed. Jennifer licked it, then rolled it between her thumb and first finger to ensure the fibers were tightly coupled together. Retrieving the needle, Jennifer turned the needle carefully until she found the small thread hole. With a very steady hand, she threaded the needle on the first try.

She could hear pages turning.

She began making the stitches that would define the leaves.

Jennifer finished the current quilt square, carefully releasing it from the wooden hoop. She watched Scott for several minutes. She had never seen him look so serious before. His expression made her nervous. She reached down into the basket, retrieved a new square to work on and carefully framed the white square so that the rose pattern was centered in the hoop. She forced herself to concentrate on her work, not Scott.

The ten o'clock news came on the radio. Scott put his finger on the page to mark his place, then looked up briefly. "Am I keeping you up?"

"I'm a night owl, Scott, 1:00 a.m. is a normal night."

He nodded. He went back to reading.

As the evening wore on and Scott continued to read, Jennifer began to feel very guilty. She should not have given him the book so late in the evening. He was already tired. He would be very late getting home. He was reading it all because it was the polite thing to do. Guilt grew as the minutes passed.

"Scott, it's midnight."

He didn't look up. "I know."

What if he didn't like the book? The thought made her feel physically sick. He did look...grim. The book was very different from the other books in the series, and it was still rough even after the editing. He was almost done with the book. Jennifer dropped any pretext about not wanting to know what he thought. She wanted to know his reaction desperately. Setting down her embroidery, she got up and crossed the room. She sat down on the couch beside him.

He turned the last page she had written, closed the book slowly. He didn't look at her, didn't say anything.

Scott felt like his heart had just been wrenched out. There was a bit of the writer in every book. In this yet-untitled book, there was more Jennifer than Scott knew how to handle. The plot was basic. A murder. The widow hired Thomas Bradford to find out who killed her husband and why. The mystery was intriguing, well written, believable, even humorous in places.

The widow in the story haunted him. She was a minor character. She introduced the mystery, providing Thomas Bradford a logical person with whom he could discuss the case. Her grief, her loneliness, her sense of drifting eloquently spoke for Jennifer herself. The critical need for the widow to understand why her husband had died wove like a tapestry thread through the entire book.

The story was so vivid in Scott's mind that emotionally he felt he had lived through the scenes personally.

"Scott? Was it that bad?" Jennifer finally whispered, afraid to know, but more afraid of not knowing.

Scott turned toward her. Jennifer didn't understand the emotions she saw.

"The story is the best you have ever written," he reassured softly.

"Really?"

"Yes." He reached for her hands. "Come here." He gently pulled her over to him, brought her to rest against his chest. Her hands settled of their own accord against his powerful upper arms.

"I was afraid you didn't like it."

"I like it." Jennifer, her head resting against his chest, felt the words. It felt so good to be held. Scott was quiet for some time. Jennifer slowly got comfortable with being held by him, began to relax.

"I'm sorry I didn't understand how badly you miss Jerry."

Jennifer stiffened.

Scott's hands moved up from her waist to gently rub her back. "It's all there, Jennifer. The anger, the grief, the sense of drifting. The loneliness."

She didn't look up at him. "It's fiction."

"No it's not."

Jennifer finally decided not to hide from him. "No it's not," she softly admitted. She sighed. "If anything, I toned down the emotions."

His hands gently slid up to shoulders that were in tense knots. "Tell me about the day Jerry died."

"Peter, what are you doing back so early?" Jennifer glanced around briefly when she heard footsteps, then turned back to the oven. "Couldn't you get a court?" She set down the cookie tray she had pulled from the oven, reaching for the spatula. "Is Jerry putting the car away? I promised him the first batch of cookies."

"Jennifer." At the broken tone in her brother's voice, Jenni-

fer looked up. She set down the spatula. "What's wrong, Peter?" she asked, fear gripping her heart.

"It's Jerry."

She leaned against the counter for support, burning her finger when it pressed against the cookie sheet.

"He had a heart attack, Jennifer."

The past tense didn't make any sense.

"He's dead, Jennifer." The blank whiteness on her brother's face told her of his own shock.

He couldn't be talking about her Jerry. They had tickets to a concert tonight. "Which hospital are they taking him to? I've got to get there." Jennifer pulled over her purse. "Memorial? Lake Forest? Condell? Where are my car keys? I need my car keys."

Her brother gripped her shoulders. "Jennifer, there were two doctors there when he collapsed. There was nothing that could be done. Jerry collapsed as we were walking down the hall to the locker rooms to get ready for our racquetball game. He suffered a massive heart attack. He died instantly."

His words began to sink in. A sob ripped through her. "Don't say that. Which hospital is he at?"

Peter shook her slightly, his own fear making his eyes almost black. "Heather is on her way. So is Pastor Kline. Don't go to pieces on me, Jennifer. Think about Colleen."

"God, you can't do this!" The cry came from the back of her throat.

Peter held her tightly. "Jerry loved you. Don't forget that honey."

"Then how can he just leave?" Jennifer practically screamed. "If he loves me, he wouldn't leave. He didn't say goodbye, Peter." Her voice dropped to a whimper. "He didn't say goodbye."

The tears began to flow unchecked. "Peter, he won't get to see Colleen. What is my little girl going to do without a father?"

The agony inside brought sobs to tear at her heart. "She won't get to grow up around her father. More than anything in the world, Jerry wanted to rock his baby girl to sleep in that rocking chair he bought."

Peter's tears silently matched hers. "I know, Jennifer. I know."

Jennifer told Scott some of the story. What she could put into words without breaking into tears.

Tell him about Colleen. The desire was there, but not the courage. She would not be able to control the tears, and she did not want to cry in front of this man, not tonight.

"I felt...*numb* I guess is the best word. There were lots of people here that night. My brother and his wife. Friends from the church Jerry and I attended. Beth and her husband Les arrived late that night. I was tired by the time that evening came, it didn't really sink in that Jerry was not coming home."

Jennifer watched her finger trace along Scott's arm following the pattern in his shirt. "Peter took care of the arrangements for me. He had gone through the details only the year before when our parents were killed."

Scott carefully brushed away the hair from her face. "When did it begin to hit you, Jennifer, that Jerry was not coming back?"

"When I saw him in that casket." Her voice broke. "We went early to have a private visitation before people began to come. It was the first time I had seen him since the morning when he left." Jennifer wasn't brave enough to tell him the rest. *The last thing he said to me was "Take care of Colleen." And he kissed me. Then he left with Peter.*

She drew in a deep breath. "The funeral was rough. By that time I was exhausted, going through the motions. But not much of it really touched me. I don't remember what the funeral service itself was like. I do remember the carnations and mums. I hate the smell of those flowers now," she said intensely. *And I was sick. The stress making my morning sickness return so strong I couldn't keep anything down. The doctors wanted to admit me to the hospital, but I wouldn't let them.*

"The first night after everyone finally left, when the house was silent, I remember standing by the window. After an hour I realized what I was doing was waiting for Jerry to come home. I went to bed alone, and I lay watching the ceiling until it was time to get up again." She gave a grim smile. "I didn't think it was possible to cry for a month. I found out I was wrong."

Scott's arms tightened around her waist. Jennifer forced the story ahead a year, determined not to talk about the rest of it. "Once that first year was past, it got easier to come home to an empty house."

"You decided to stay here?"

"Yes. Peter and Heather wanted me to move in with them, but I declined. This house is lonely now, but it's still home. Little things Jerry and I did to make it fit us, the bird feeders in the backyard, the hammock we used all the time. I can't walk away from this place."

Scott rubbed his chin across the top of her head. "I'm very sorry you lost your husband, Jennifer. He sounds like he was a good man."

She nodded. "You would have liked him, I think."

Scott gently touched the dark circles under her eyes. "You still miss him a lot, don't you?"

"Yes." Jennifer pulled away from his arms to lean back against the couch. "I don't understand it, Scott. But I think about Jerry more now than I did a year ago. The memories are strong, almost painful, at times, they are so clear."

"Because of the book?"

"Maybe. When I eventually finished the book Jerry and I had been working on together when he died, I was pretty much caught in my 'I'm mad at you' stage. I had a very severe case of depression, Why had life dared to change on me? I was well past that when I began this book. When I started writing this book, it was more a matter of learning to live a new life without Jerry. If my life was going on, how did I want to live it if I was alone? I keep remembering the past, how good it was, the fun we had together. I can't see anything in the future that will compare with the past, and that is a very dangerous position to be in."

"You loved your husband," Scott replied, understanding.

Jennifer smiled. "With a passion." She sighed. "Really loving someone means being willing to let them die first. That was the most difficult lesson I have ever had to learn." Jennifer rubbed her eyes.

Jerry, I hope you like holding our daughter. I failed you. Failed Colleen. And God failed me. One simple prayer, Lord. Why couldn't you answer that one simple, specific prayer?

"Scott, it's late. Hadn't you better be going?"

Scott could see the pain still in her eyes. He knew she was closing the subject before she had told him all of it. But it would do no good to push. It would only cause more pain; he wanted to help ease her pain, not make it worse. There would be other nights. "Yes, I suppose I should." He reached out a hand to gently touch hers. "Thank you, Jennifer."

She smiled. "I still think you should go away and come back in a year."

He returned her smile, replying seriously, "I don't."

He touched the three-ring binder as he got to his feet. "Thanks for letting me read your book. I really did like it."

Jennifer got to her feet. "I'm glad." She carried the book over to the desk.

They walked together through the quiet house to the front door. "Are we still on for Thursday night, Jennifer?"

She nodded. "Yes."

He smiled. "Good. Get some sleep."

"I will. Drive carefully, Scott."

Jennifer shut the door after him, then leaned wearily against the door. The emotions of what she had not told him sent two solitary tears running down her cheeks.

"God, help me."

The prayer was broken, painful, so much emotion sitting beneath the surface. She was petrified of how Scott would react if he saw the pain. She couldn't show it to anyone, not Peter, not Rachel, only a little of it to Beth. They thought she had grieved for her husband and daughter and had begun to move on. The fact she had not only made her misery more deep. She should have grieved and moved on. But she hadn't. There was so much pain, the tears were so near the surface any time she even thought about her daughter. The wound in her heart seemed to only grow with time, not heal.

God, why didn't you answer that last prayer? Why?

She wanted to scream the words, but instead they were whispered with eyes full of tears.

Chapter Five

Jennifer was deep into writing the synopsis of the book her publisher would need for the sales and marketing departments when the phone rang. "Hello?"

"Hi, Jen."

"Scott." She put down her pen with a smile. "Hi."

"Are you going to be free after six? I would like to take you out to dinner and a movie," he asked, getting straight to the point.

"We have a date tomorrow night."

"Consider it a double feature. All I'm getting done here is creating more work. Please, give me a reason to leave."

She laughed. "I would love to," Jennifer replied, twisting the telephone cord around her fingers.

"Great. I'll pick you up about six-fifteen."

"Sounds fine. What movie?"

"I'm flexible," Scott replied. "There is a comedy, a murder mystery, three action adventures, and a Walt Disney film showing now."

"Who is in the comedy?"

"Tom Hanks."

"Let's see the comedy."

"Done. See you after six."

Scott was early. Jennifer was trying to fasten her left earring when the doorbell rang. She was wearing dress slacks and a light sweater, but the earrings were her absolute favorites, and she was determined to wear them. Her mother had given them to her on her twenty-first birthday.

Carrying the earring, she went to get the door. "Hi, Scott. Come on in. I won't be but a minute."

He smiled. "Take your time. I'm early."

She retreated to the bedroom. "Did the rest of the day turn out okay?"

He came to lounge against the door frame as she finished putting on the earrings. "Tolerable. I swear the paper just grows more paper."

She grinned. "The stories feel like that sometimes." She began looking for her shoes.

"They are under the bed, Jennifer," he commented, having spotted the black flats.

She pulled out the shoes. "Thanks."

"If you have a jacket, I would recommend you grab it."

Jennifer nodded. She went to the closet to retrieve her leather jacket. "I don't have anything lighter. I left my windbreaker at Peter's."

"This is perfect. You may need it before the night is over."

"Just what do you have planned?"

He held up his hands. "Just dinner and a movie. But it's good to be prepared."

She grinned. "Oh."

He smiled softly. "You're in a good mood tonight."

"Quite a change, isn't it?" She smiled, offered a slight shrug. "The book is about ready to go to Ann."

"Does that imply that when the writing is not going so well, you're not in a great mood?"

"How do you feel after a day dealing with one crisis after another?"

"Touché." He smiled. "You and Jerry had a warning system, didn't you? A way to tell the other when it had been a lousy day on the book."

She nodded. "If I told him to order in pizza, he got the message. Jerry," she grinned, "he would unwind by practicing on his trumpet."

"Was he good?"

Jennifer chuckled. "No." She picked up her purse. "Okay, Scott, I'm ready."

He locked the house for her. "Any preference tonight?"

"How about something Mexican?"

Scott held the passenger door for her. "I know the perfect place. About fifteen minutes from here." Rounding the car, he took the driver's seat. They left the subdivision. "I'm glad you decided to come tonight."

"So am I."

He looked over at her, shared a smile.

"Scott, you're driving. Your eyes are supposed to be on the road," Jennifer reminded him.

"You're a distraction."

"Of course I am. Watch the road," she replied with a grin.

The restaurant was a small place, tucked out of the general flow of traffic on a side street. "You'll like this place, Jennifer. It has great food." He offered her a hand from the car. As they walked to the door, his arm came firmly around her waist. He had not forgotten what she said about first times.

"Watch the number of hot peppers beside the name of the dish. They will tell you how hot and spicy it is," Scott warned her when they were seated.

Jennifer nodded. She read the menu with interest. "Everything looks delicious, Scott."

He smiled. "It is."

Jennifer finally settled on the burritos, extra spicy.

"You like hot and spicy?" Scott asked, surprised.

"I love it," Jennifer replied, raiding the bowl of taco chips the restaurant offered as a courtesy. They were homemade. And delicious.

Scott placed the order for both of them. He had chosen the same dish as Jennifer. "Try some of this." He pushed the bowl of hot salsa over to her.

"Not bad." Jennifer replied after a couple of samples.

Scott smiled. "Are you going to continually surprise me like this, Jennifer?"

"Doesn't everyone like spicy food?"

He chuckled. "No." He offered the chip he held. Hers had broken in the dish.

"Thanks. I've only known you a few weeks," she commented.

"That's significant?"

She nodded. "I've already seen you four times. This makes five. Tomorrow will make six."

"And?"

"Just how much are you planning for us to try and pack into this month?"

"Just as much as you'll let me."

"I was afraid of that. You look tired, Scott."

"A little."

"It's not good to rush this, you know."

"I know."

"So how come we're doing this?"

He grinned. "Because it really was the best idea I had all day." He lifted another chip and offered it to her. She took a bite.

Dinner arrived.

"Tell me about these Monday-night football games. How long have you and Peter been getting together?"

"Jerry started it. He and Peter were close friends almost from the day they met. Monday night became the guys' night out." She smiled at the memory. "Peter used to always come early, and they would disappear somewhere for dinner, play a little basketball in the church gymnasium. Jerry was the coach for the church team for a while, then they would come back to the house in time to catch the game. I invariably ended up on the couch with Jerry for the duration of the game." She chuckled. "He got an elbow in his ribs a couple times when he distracted me from the game. I love football, always have."

She hesitated. "After Jerry's death, Monday night was a way for Peter and me to both keep part of his memory alive. Peter uses it as an excuse to come over, see how I'm doing."

Scott was glad she was willing to share with him her life with Jerry. It mattered. It meant she was trusting him with the most important part of who she was. He wanted to understand her past. He needed to understand her past. "That takes courage Jennifer, to hold on to the good memories rather than to try to bury all the memories, good and bad."

"Maybe. As time goes on, the Monday nights have become easier. Those first few months, they were not so enjoyable." Jennifer sighed. "Peter blamed himself for Jerry's death. There was absolutely no reason to, but because he was the one with him, he felt like he should have been able to do something. I was afraid for a long time that I had lost my brother as well as my husband. Peter takes guilt very seriously. And there were some extenuating circumstances which didn't help." Like Colleen.

"What brought him around?"

"I yelled at him a few times. And he was worried about me. Had to be around to protect me. Time wore away the edge of the pain."

Jennifer needed the subject changed. "Tell me about your sister, Scott. What's she like?"

Scott followed her lead. "Heather? She is unique. Quiet. Shy. Has vivid blue eyes." He smiled. "Very strong willed. She knew who she was, what she wanted to do from the time she was five. Flowers. Anything she did was going to revolve around flowers."

"You said she's a florist now?"

"Yes. And has a thriving greenhouse business. She can make literally anything grow." He spun the ice in his glass, looked over at her. "I have to confess something. I stood Heather up in order to take you to the play *Chess*. That's why I'm on the hook to introduce you two."

Jennifer laughed. "Scott, you didn't!"

"I did," he admitted.

"How long a lecture did she give you?"

He smiled. "An earful. I told her you had pretty eyes. It quieted her down."

Jennifer had not laughed so much in months. "Scott, not while I'm this full," she protested. "Now how am I supposed to meet your sister tomorrow night without being nervous?"

"You two will get along just fine."

The waiter stopped to inquire if they would be interested

in any dessert. Jennifer declined with a smile. Scott asked for the check. "The movie starts in about thirty minutes. It's time we headed over there."

He reached for her hand as they left the restaurant.

The movie theater was crowded. Scott bought their tickets, escorted Jennifer through the crowds both entering and leaving the theater. He gestured toward the refreshment stand. "Want some popcorn?"

Jennifer laughed at his hopeful expression. "And a large diet cola," she added.

He smiled. "Okay. Any candy?"

"Maybe an ice-cream cone after the movie," Jennifer said.

He nodded. Regretfully he let go of her hand. "No need for you to stand in this mob. I'll meet you by the doors to Theater Three?"

Jennifer nodded. "You won't need a hand?"

"I'll manage. See you soon." He went to find a place in line.

Jennifer made her way to Theater Three. She frowned. There were children everywhere. The Disney film was showing in Theater Four. She forced herself to take a deep breath. She started reading movie posters, anything to keep from looking at the children.

A little hand pulled at the fabric of Jennifer's slacks. "Hi." The child was holding a handful of bright red licorice sticks. "Would you like one?"

The girl could be at best three years old. Jennifer felt physically sick. Blond hair. Brown eyes. Dark eyelashes. A perfect grin. The girl could have been her own daughter had she lived. "Thank you, honey, but I already have a treat." Jennifer held up the piece of wrapped candy she had been carrying since they left the restaurant.

"Okay."

"Mandy, come over here beside Mommy."

The little girl turned. Jennifer looked up to see a lady carrying an infant coming toward them. The lady offered an apologetic smile on behalf of her daughter. Jennifer offered a soft envious smile is return. The little girl tottered off happily toward her mother.

The pain tore into her gut, and her heart stopped beating momentarily, held in the grip of a tight fist. Her composure already shaken, the encounter was enough to tip the balance. Lord, get me out of here. It was a desperate plea, and Jennifer was already turning to find the exit when Scott joined her. Never had she been more happy to see someone than at that moment. "Scott, would you please take me home?" She was desperate, and it came across in her voice and her eyes.

"Jennifer, what's wrong?" He set down the popcorn and drinks on the ledge of a display. She looked pale, shaky on her feet. He hadn't realized she wasn't feeling well.

"I need to leave," she replied softly, forcefully.

Kicking himself for not being more observant, Scott abandoned the food and maneuvered them toward the exit. Now was not the time for questions. Concern became alarm as they passed a family with an infant and a blond-haired little girl. Jennifer looked like she was going to pass out. His arm around her waist tightened. They reached the doors and she wobbled on her feet. "Let's get your jacket on, Jennifer," he said, quickly pulling it apart from his. She rested her head against the cold glass, letting him slip her jacket around her shoulders. He hurriedly found his keys.

Colleen. She tried to fight the tears. Didn't succeed.

His hand gripped hers. "Jennifer?"

She just shook her head.

Scott wrapped his arm firmly around her waist and

pushed open the door. He was grateful they had parked nearby. Unlocking the passenger door, he helped her inside. Quickly, he moved around to the driver's seat. She was shivering. He started the car and turned the heater on full blast.

She took a painful breath and let it out slowly.

He watched her closely. There was very little color in her face, and her jaw was clenched as she tried to fight the tears. He'd never seen someone in shock before, and that was what he was seeing. "What happened?"

She turned her head against the seat to look at him, and it was obvious she didn't want to tell him, didn't know how to apologize for her request, didn't know what to say. "An old memory, Scott. I just wasn't ready for it," she finally said painfully.

Pain? This was agony. His hand reached over to comfortably grip hers. "Want to tell me about it?" Please, have the courage to tell me, he prayed silently.

How do I tell him about Colleen? Jennifer struggled to find the words and simply could not. The tears were already falling. To open up that pain would be devastating right now. "I'm sorry, Scott. I just can't."

If her refusal hurt, he didn't show it. He gently pulled her over from leaning against the door. His arms came around her and, very softly, he leaned down and brushed a kiss against her forehead. "It's okay, Jennifer," he said quietly, and the gentleness in his voice, his touch, told her the rest. He really was willing to give her the freedom to decide when and if she told him what was wrong. Scott kept her tucked close against his side and pulled the car out into traffic.

"Have you ever seen the city lights from Overlook Drive?" He asked a few minutes later when her tears had quieted.

She shook her head.

"They are worth seeing," Scott commented, looking down at her with a question in his eyes.

Jennifer was grateful he was not ending the evening early. She wouldn't have blamed him if he had. "I would like to see them, Scott." She rested her head against his shoulder. The arm around her moved, brushed the hair away from her face, before setting back around shoulders. "Close your eyes. Rest. We are several minutes from Overlook Drive. I'll let you know before we get there."

Jennifer could feel Scott's words as well as hear them. The last time she had been this close to a man was with Jerry. She had missed it. She closed her eyes, more than willing to just enjoy being beside him, to dream a bit about it being for real, permanent. Anything to stop her from thinking about Colleen. "These memories are never going to fade, Scott."

His arm tightened. "Yes, they will."

"How?"

"They get replaced. Eventually, they get replaced."

She sighed. "I sometimes wish I had never met Jerry."

"Jennifer."

"Okay, more accurately, I wish he had not died."

Scott knew she needed to talk. "How did you meet Jerry?"

He felt her smile. "English class. He was good-looking, out-going. A journalism major. After class, eight of us were sitting at a table in the cafeteria, eating popcorn, studying. He joined us, taking the seat across from me. Introduced himself. Said he had seen me in class. Asked what my major was. Grinned, and asked what I wanted to be when I grew up. I finally got together the nerve to admit I wanted to be a writer. He didn't joke about it. His blue eyes got serious. 'Really?'" Jennifer smiled again. "I could tell he was impressed, Scott. He asked what I had written, which was not much at the time."

Scott chuckled. "Tell me the rest of it, Jennifer," he encouraged.

"He chose me as his study partner. He didn't need a study partner. He was smarter than I was. I liked his company. After a week and a half of his company every day, I stopped being shy around him. I liked him. He was the head of the campus Christian fellowship. He introduced me to half of the campus within the first week and a half.

"The lecture halls at college were like theaters, the wooden rows of seats angled up. I liked the tenth row in the middle. The professor couldn't see what you were doing, but it was not the back of the auditorium, either. Jerry would toss his backpack of books onto the chair beside me, offer a good morning, then mingle, saying hi to half the class before the professor arrived. A minute before class began, he would drop into the seat beside me with a smile.

"Our lit class was the first class of the day. Jerry would bring the day's newspaper to class. I never took notes during class. I just listened to the lecture. Jerry took lots of notes. It was a two-hour class. The newspaper would come out quietly about twenty minutes into class.

"I had the habit of writing late into the night. I often slept until the last minute before racing to class. More than once I brought breakfast of a danish to class. By the third week, bringing both of us a danish was the rule."

Jennifer savored the memory of those carefree days. "Jerry soon figured out that my green notebook was my story notebook. He would see it come out, and he would offer a grin. He never read over my shoulder. That surprised me. It certainly made life easier. I didn't like most of what I wrote until the fourth or fifth draft. If I liked the story, I would slip the notebook over to him. He was like Beth. He liked everything I wrote. If I asked how I could make a story better, he would think about it awhile, then offer a different way the plot might develop, or a way to make a character more striking. Jerry loved a good mystery."

"Did you write your first book together?"

Jennifer nodded. "The sixth week of class I brought a special notebook to lit class. Asked him to read it. It was the first seventy pages of what turned out to be our first book. I had created private eye Thomas Bradford the year before, and the story had slowly evolved. Jerry was so thrilled by the book he came looking for me at the dorm. He had never come inside the dorm before. He wanted to know when I was going to finish the story. I was astounded that he liked it. I didn't think it was that good. When I told him I didn't know how it was going to end, he really got upset. He wanted to know how the case was solved, and I hadn't figured that out yet."

Scott laughed. "Is that when he got involved?"

Jennifer nodded. "He bugged me about the book for weeks. I finally told him if he wanted the book finished he was going to have to help me with it. He took me at my word. Tuesday, Wednesday and Friday afternoons he would drag me down to the bagel place, pick out a corner booth, buy us a late lunch, and we would sort out what had to happen in the book next. He started meeting me at my dorm and walking with me to lit class so he could read what I had written the night before."

Jennifer turned her wedding ring around. "I fell in love with Jerry that semester," she said softly.

"You have good memories, Jennifer. Be glad for that."

"I am. I just want those times back so badly, the memories hurt."

"They were all good times?"

Jennifer thought about it. "No," she admitted. "I was

petrified I would not be able to sell my book," she said smiling, "petrified that I would. Worried about Jerry and what he thought of me."

With a great deal of reluctance Scott told her, "We are almost at Overlook Drive. When we reach the top of this rise, you will be able to see the city lights spread out below us."

Jennifer, with an equal amount of reluctance, sat up. And then she caught sight of the view. "Scott, this is incredible." The city was spread out before them, lights twinkling in a shimmering darkness.

"It helps to have a clear night." He pulled into the overlook. "Care to get out?"

She nodded. Scott turned off the car. Jennifer stepped out and slipped her jacket on properly. Scott went around the car to stop beside her. He leaned against the hood.

"I am surprised there are so many colors to the city lights," Jennifer remarked.

"Do you see the spotlight? There to the right?"

"What is it? A hospital?"

"Probably."

Jennifer smiled. "It looks like a lighthouse beacon." She leaned back beside him. "It's a nice night for seeing the stars."

"Know your constellations?"

"The Big Dipper. That is about it."

"Same here," Scott admitted. He leaned his hands back against the hood of the car to look up. "It's an awesome sight."

"Very," Jennifer agreed. She touched his arm. "You can see the Milky Way over there."

"Maybe someday we will understand the magnitude of what we are looking at."

"Maybe."

Scott looked over, hearing the shiver in her voice. "You're cold. Let's finish the drive."

She nodded. "I'm glad we stopped."

"So am I."

They drove along the mile drive slowly. The road began to descend. "Thanks, Scott. I enjoyed that."

He smiled. "So did I." He glanced at the clock on the dashboard. "It's just going on ten. We are near my place. Would you like some coffee?"

"Please."

It had been a pleasant drive, Jennifer thought.

"Jerry and I used to come to this beach years ago. He loved the water," Jennifer commented as they drove along the lake toward Scott's home. She thought about those days and closed her eyes, fighting the sadness the memories brought.

Scott's hand reached over to hold hers.

"Make yourself comfortable, I'll be right back with the coffee," Scott said, escorting her into the living room of his home. It had a cathedral ceiling and was full of plants, beautiful pictures and comfortable furniture. She took a seat on one of the couches where she would have a good view out the windows. The moon was visible now. Almost full. Hanging low on the horizon.

"You look beautiful tonight." Jerry's arms came around his wife from behind, encircling the white, soft fuzzy robe she wore.

She smiled and leaned back against him. "Thanks," she said softly, but her attention didn't shift from the view. "You can see the sailboats in the harbor when the moonlight hits the masts just right."

"You're right," he said after a minute.

"I love this view."

"So do I."

Jennifer blushed. Her husband had turned his attention back to her.

"Did I pick a good spot for a honeymoon?"

"Perfect." She linked her hands with his. "Could we go sailing tomorrow?"

"Already planned."

"Jennifer."

She broke out of her reverie to accept the china cup. "Thank you."

He took a seat beside her, stretched his legs out.

"We had a view like this on our honeymoon. A big full moon. The soft smell of the ocean in the air," Jennifer said softly.

Scott tilted his head to look over at her. "Where did you go?"

"Northern Washington state. A little town on the coast." Jennifer carefully tasted the hot coffee. A very faint taste of cinnamon. It was good. She leaned her head back against the high-backed couch. "You would like being married, Scott." She knew he was heading that way. It was written all over him. This man wanted to find a wife. The possibility was hard to consider. They were at different points in their lives, and sometime soon he was going to need to accept that and move on. She couldn't consider a second marriage. Not now. Not with so much grief so raw inside.

"What were those years like, Jennifer?"

Jennifer tried to give him a word picture of those years. "Morning devotions. Notes on the refrigerator. Constant deadlines. Tired eyes. Hard work. Libraries. Books. Lots of books. Late nights. Lazy afternoons. Chili dogs and baseball games. Naps in the hammock. Good books. Good movies. Good pizza. Raking leaves. Football games. Chocolate chip cookies. Hot cider. Hugs. Fires in the fireplace. Fuzzy warm blankets. Board games. Jerry cheating at cards. Christmas carols. Snowball fights. Laughter. Dinner parties. Quiet talks. No money. Lots of money. Sunny days in the park. Frisbee. Holding hands. Violets. Rainy days. Sleeping late. Breakfast in bed. Snuggling. Beautiful sunsets. Prayer. Arguments. Making up." She ran out of words.

Scott sat in silence for a long time. He had turned to watch her as she spoke, her gaze focused out on the distant lights, her attention in the past. "Describe life now, Jennifer," he asked quietly, already knowing what type of answer she was going to give. He wasn't prepared for its intensity.

"Lonely nights. Dark rooms. Tears. Anger. Lackluster meals. Being alone. Being scared. Pity in people's faces. Uncertainty. Silence. Drifting. Sadness. Broken things. Empty closets. Pity parties. Cloudy days. Shady salesmen. Bills. Isolation. Drowning. Doubting."

There was not a single thing he could say. He reached out his hand. After a moment's hesitation, she moved her own over to settle in his. His hand tightened around hers. "Thank you for answering me."

He got up and refilled her coffee. He didn't sit back down, instead moved over to lean against the window. "What plans do you have now?"

She sighed. "So many memories need to be settled. Maybe the next few months can deal with them, I don't know. I'll start on a new book."

"You're not looking forward to the change."

"I hate new things. I like comfortable, well-defined patterns. Not chaos and more uncertainty."

"Are you sure I'm not going to complicate things?"

She smiled. "Scott, you have disrupted my life from the day I met you. Of course you complicate things. But you are a nice disruption."

"Why are you so afraid of new things, Jennifer?"

She ran a hand through her hair. "I don't know. Mainly because I don't know what to do, what to say. I get flustered."

"If I throw you a first, will you at least consider it?"

She hesitantly nodded.

He walked to her side. Held out his hand. "Dance with me."

He lifted her to her feet, led her over to recessed shelves where she found a nice stereo. He slid the top CD into the player. The orchestra music filled the room. He held out his hands. Jennifer took the one step forward into his arms.

He was a good dancer. Jennifer rested her head against his chest, finding it easy to relax. "I could get used to this."

She felt him smile.

He was standing across the hall from the ladies' room, waiting for her.

He moved to her side when he saw her.

"Sorry about that," Jennifer said quietly, apologetically.

He studied her face for a moment.

"I brought you a drink. It looks like you could use it," he said finally, handing her one of the glasses he carried.

It looked like liquor. "Scott, I don't drink. Except under extreme duress," she qualified, remembering the anniversary of her husband's death.

"Neither, actually, do I. It's iced tea."

She blushed with embarrassment.

"Quit that, Jen. If you hadn't asked, I would have been upset."

Jennifer tilted her head to look at him. He was serious. She was never going to get used to this man.

Jennifer accidentally stepped on Scott's foot. It was the first time she had ever had a flashback about Scott instead of Jerry. It stunned her.

The arm at her waist tightened. "Okay?"

"Yes. Sorry," she replied, still thinking about that memory. She smiled. It was a nice memory.

The music eventually ended. Jennifer reluctantly stepped back. Scott's hand reached up to gently brush her cheek. "Thank you, Jennifer," he said seriously.

She wisely said nothing.

"It's late. I should get you home."

The lake was quiet, still, steam rising with the dawn. Scott let the boat drift in toward the shore. With a smooth motion he cast out toward his right. He had been on the lake for an hour now, and the fish were striking at anything that flickered across the top of the water. He began smoothly reeling the lure back toward the boat waiting to feel the strike of a bass.

Jennifer was the one. Jennifer was the lady he wanted to marry.

It was a gut-level decision that he was making, but it felt right, it felt solid. He liked her. He liked her a lot. Okay, in truth, he was falling in love with her. He liked the idea of being married to a writer. He liked her personality and her preference for silence. He liked the sound of her voice. He could envision her being in his life twenty years from now.

She would make a great mom. Scott smiled as he thought about it, thought about what Jennifer was like when she talked about her niece, Tiffany, so much pride in her voice, so much love. He would love to have children with Jennifer. Two, maybe three children to fill his house. He would love to be called Dad. He could teach them to waterski, teach them to fish, teach them to love books and learning, teach them to love cooking. It was going to be great being a dad.

He couldn't wait for Heather to meet her. His mom and dad were going to love her.

Yes, Jennifer was the right one. She was perfect for him, an answer to his prayer.

Chapter Six

The last thing Jennifer felt like doing was spending an evening with Scott, going to dinner and meeting his sister. The argument she had had with God the night before had taken its toll. She wanted answers, and they were not being given. Her head was pounding. She had been in a rotten mood all day. She looked at the run in her hose. With a sigh she tossed the silk nylons into the wastebasket.

The mirror above the bathroom sink gave her a good picture of just how awful she looked.

She knew after a day of thinking about it that she had crossed the line from being honest to being disrespectful last night. God allowed her the right to be honest, to question him, to even be angry with Him, but being disrespectful was not acceptable and she knew it.

She looked up at the ceiling. "God, I am sorry."

Jennifer looked at herself in the mirror. Grimaced. She pulled her hair back into a ponytail, reached for a washcloth.

When Scott arrived an hour later, he found a very subdued Jennifer sitting in the living room watching for him to arrive. Her dress was a beautiful sapphire blue, a simple, striking dress. Scott looked her over with pleasure. "I like it."

She smiled, his compliment helping assuage a very wounded spirit. She had discarded almost her entire wardrobe trying to find something which would not accentuate her pallor. Scott's second careful study of her face told her she had not totally hidden the effects of the day. The hand that took hers was gentle. "What's wrong?"

"I had a rough day," she admitted. "A lot on my mind."

"Would you like to take a pass on tonight? All you have to do is say the word."

"No. I'm okay. Just a little tired."

He nodded, understanding better than she realized that she really was emotionally exhausted. Her eyes told a message of their own. "We'll make it an early evening," he said.

He helped her on with her coat and locked the door for her.

Jennifer was surprised, at the same time relieved, by Scott's willingness to let the silence stretch between them. He had slipped a cassette into the player; the soft piano music was the only sound in the car.

Jennifer watched him as he drove. He really was a very handsome man. She now knew him well enough to be able to see the smile lines around his eyes, the little brush of silver-gray in his hair. She had found him in the past few weeks to be solid, dependable, trustworthy, gentle. A man who understood how to care, how to support. She had thought, after first meeting him, that he would be a man she would feel smothered being around. That the strength of his own personality would overwhelm her. Instead, she found him a very comfortable man to be around. He had never threatened her own carefully protected space. He listened. Let her choose how much to say. He was not threatened by silence.

He looked over and caught her inspection. Smiled with a question in his eyes. She shook her head slightly, her thoughts not something she could put into words. His smile deepened, but he chose not to break the silence.

The restaurant Scott chose surprised Jennifer. French. Quiet. Elegant. Their table, tucked in the corner, very private. Jennifer found herself on uncertain ground. She looked over at Scott.

His smile was gentle. "Relax, Jennifer. It's going to be a quiet evening, nothing more."

His soft reassurance made her blush with embarrassment.

"Stop that, Jennifer," he said, his voice suddenly stern, his hand reaching over to grasp hers. "Caution does not warrant an apology."

"It does if it's unfounded."

"No, it doesn't." He released her hand. "Please, Jennifer, trust me. You don't have to apologize for being cautious."

She lowered her eyes. "Thank you, Scott."

He frowned. "Jennifer, what happened today? Something is seriously wrong."

She looked up. The waiter joining them to take their orders, gave her a reason not to answer immediately. Their orders given, once again alone, Jennifer looked over at Scott and debated how to answer him. "I had a fight with God," she finally admitted.

His serious expression told her how strongly he took that news.

"It's not the first one we have had, nor will it likely be the last one. But the aftereffects are difficult to deal with."

"Why, Jennifer?"

"Scott, there is a great deal you don't know about me. I don't know that I can explain everything that is going on. I am still at odds with God over some basic issues involving Jerry." She sighed. "I pushed my case on one of those issues last night."

"Are you okay, Jennifer?"

"He's my Father, Scott. I don't like being at odds with Him. But I don't understand Him at times, and it is not an easy position to be in. It's just going to take some time to resolve."

"Jennifer, do you want to talk about the issues? I'll help if I can."

I would have to tell you about Colleen. I don't want you to see that side of me, Scott, that angry, hurting side of me. There is a limit to what a new relationship can support. I can't share that level of grief. Not yet. She reached over to touch his hand. "Thank you, Scott. I will take you up on that offer sometime. I can't tonight."

He squeezed her hand. "It's an open offer, Jennifer."

Dinner arrived. They both kept the conversation light during dinner, away from emotional subjects. Jennifer began to relax. By the end of the meal, Scott had succeeded in making her laugh several times. "Thank you, Scott," she said softly, gratefully, as they crossed the parking lot.

He hugged her. "That's what friends are for, Jennifer." He held the car door for her, closing it softly once she had slipped inside.

"Would you rather pass on meeting Heather tonight?"

It was a tempting offer. "No, Scott. Let's get it over with."

He smiled. "You don't have to be so nervous about this, Jennifer. Heather promised to be on her best behavior."

She's pregnant, Scott. That's the real problem. Jennifer forced a smile. "She's your sister, Scott."

"Don't hold it against her. As she so often says, she didn't have a choice in the matter."

Jennifer laughed. "Okay, Scott."

It was a thirty-minute drive to Heather and Frank's home. The house was two stories with white siding and a van parked in the driveway. As Jennifer expected, the yard was beautifully landscaped. The porch light was on. Scott pulled into the driveway behind the van.

Scott put a comforting arm around Jennifer's waist as they walked toward the front door. The door opened within moments of Scott ringing the doorbell. Heather's husband, Frank. "Scott. Jennifer. Welcome. Please, come in." Frank held the door for them with a smile.

"Jennifer, this is my sister's husband, Frank." Scott did the introductions once they were inside.

"Hello, Frank," Jennifer said with a nervous smile.

Frank took her hand. "It's nice to finally meet you, Jennifer. Let me take your coats. Come in and make yourselves comfortable. Heather's on her way down. The kids are already in bed."

The living room was beautiful. White carpet. Bold red, green and blue fabrics for the two love seats, the easy chairs. Scott's hand on her waist, warm through the fabric of her dress, was a comforting guide.

"Scott! I am sorry. I was working in the nursery."

Jennifer didn't need to be told this was Heather. The lady was very petite, at most five feet two inches. She carried being pregnant beautifully. Scott met her with a hug. "Hi, Twig." He smiled at the paint splatters on her face. "Let me guess...you're working on the forest."

"Yes." She rubbed at the offending paint drops, her attention already turning to her guest. Scott reached back for Jennifer's hand.

"Jennifer, this is my sister, Heather. Heather, Jennifer St. James."

"Hi," Heather said softly, her natural shyness competing with an intense interest in Scott's new friend.

Jennifer bravely smiled in return. "Hello, Heather."

Both men were quick to step in to ease the tension. "Jennifer, Scott, would you like some coffee?" Frank asked.

"Please," Scott replied for both of them. "Heather, sit down, get off your feet. We won't stay long. How is the nursery coming?" Scott settled Jennifer on the love seat beside him, his fingers interlacing with hers, which were surprisingly cold.

"I'm almost halfway done with the forest," Heather replied. "I've been painting a mural around the nursery, something to make it different...not just white walls," she explained for Jennifer's benefit.

Jennifer found if she looked at Heather's face she could keep her nerves under control. "Did you create the design yourself, or are you using stencils?" she asked, working hard to keep her voice steady.

"Stencils. I found them in a children's book and then enlarged them."

Jennifer was intrigued. "Does the mural cover the entire wall?"

Heather grinned. "Yes. Frank gets to paint the part by the floor."

Frank came back in carrying a tray of coffee cups. He handed them around. A black Samoyed followed him into the room.

"Hi, Blackie." Scott greeted the dog.

"She's beautiful." The dog came over to say hello. Jennifer ran her hand along the warm fur of the dog's back.

"Would you like to see her puppies, Jennifer?" Heather offered.

"Yes, I would."

Heather waved both her husband and her brother back to their seats. "Stay put, we won't be long."

Scott felt the flutter in Jennifer's pulse. He gently squeezed her hand as she got up. The ladies left the room, walked through the house to the back patio where a small greenhouse had been built.

"Sorry, Jennifer, but it's rather difficult to talk about my brother when he's in the room. How do you like him so far?"

Jennifer chuckled. Heather was perfect. "I like him, Heather."

Heather smiled. "Good." She held open the door to the greenhouse. "The puppies have a home out here for the time being." She turned on the overhead lights. The room was warm, smelled moist, of earth, foliage and the fragrant smell of flowers.

Jennifer followed Heather slowly, captivated by the plants, the flowers, the violets. Jennifer stopped to carefully touch the leaves of a beautiful purple flowering violet.

"Do you like it? It's one of my personal favorites."

"I love it."

"I'll send you a couple of plants home. All they need is sunlight and water and they thrive."

Jennifer grimaced. "I just killed my last violets. The flowers around my porch are surviving by pure luck. I am not known for my ability to care for anything that is green."

Heather chuckled. "You can learn. Look at Scott. The man could turn anything brown within a week, but he's gotten better with time."

"Scott actually waters plants?"

Heather laughed. "You would be surprised."

The four puppies were curled up together on a quilt in a big basket, all sleeping.

"Heather, they are adorable." Jennifer gently stroked the soft fur of the two nearest puppies.

"I think so. The kids love them." Heather picked up the nearest puppy. "This is Pepper. He has the only markings in the litter. Two white feet."

Jennifer chuckled. "Cute. What are the others' names?"

"The nearest one is Choc, short for chocolate, then Gretta, and finally Quigley."

Jennifer reached across to stroke the last puppy. He woke enough to open his eyes, lick her hand. "Who thought up the name Quigley?"

Heather grinned. "Scott. He's planning to adopt him when he gets a few weeks older."

"He will have his hands full."

Heather set Pepper back down on the quilt. "Yes, he will." Heather groaned softly as she straightened.

"When's your baby due?"

"Eight more weeks. Would you like to see the nursery, Jennifer?"

Jennifer wanted to decline. Part of her also wanted to run the risk. She was curious to see what Heather had done with the nursery, see the mural. She took a chance. "Yes I would."

Heather led them back inside, up to the second floor.

Jennifer hesitated in the doorway to the room, then forced herself to cross the threshold. The room was lovely. The furniture had been shifted to one side of the room to leave the wall with the mural open. Jennifer looked around the room. "Heather, I love it." She could tell the colors had been carefully chosen to favor neither pink nor blue. "Do you know if you are going to have a boy or a girl?"

"No. We decided we would rather wait."

Jennifer smiled. "Do you have a preference?"

"Not a strong one. As long as my baby is healthy, I will be happy. I already know the delivery will have to be a cesarean-section. My rebuilt right hip will not allow a normal delivery. I'm not looking forward to that."

"If it's going to be necessary, at least you know from the beginning. To go through hours of labor and then have to have a C-section would be awful."

Heather groaned. "That is an understatement."

"I love the curtains, Heather. Did you make them yourself?"

"Mom made them for me."

"This will be their third grandchild?"

"Yes. Scott has disappointed Mom, she always hoped he would be the first to have a family."

Jennifer absorbed that remark, tucking it away as confirmation of something she already suspected. She walked over to study the mural design. If she looked closely, she could see the design yet to be painted penciled on the wall. "This looks very intricate."

"It is taking much longer than I originally planned. The leaves are so detailed."

"There's a leopard," Jennifer said in surprise, finding the penciled figure in the mural.

Heather joined her, carefully tracing the penciled figure. "He is going to be so key to the mural that I haven't yet had the nerve to begin painting him."

Jennifer nodded. "At least you have lots of leaves to practice on."

Heather smiled. "Exactly."

Eventually, after inspecting everything in the room, discussing future plans for furniture and colors, they left the nursery together. "How did you like the play?" Heather asked as they made their way back downstairs.

"I loved it. Scott told me he stood you up."

Heather laughed. "I forgave him. At least he was not using work as an excuse this time."

"Is it just a wrong impression, or does Scott work too hard?"

Heather considered the question carefully. "He's the first one in our family to reach such an important position, I don't really have a reference to say what is normal for a position such as his. I know he doesn't relax easily, that the job is always there weighing on his mind. He has to continually struggle to have a life away from his job."

Jennifer nodded thoughtfully. "Thanks, Heather."

"Sure. Scott tells me you recently finished another book?"

"Yes."

"I've read all of your books. You're a very good writer, Jennifer."

"Thank you," Jennifer said, caught off guard.

Heather grinned. "Don't be so modest. I envy you your talent. One of these days, we need to go to lunch together. I would love to hear what it's like to be a writer."

Jennifer laughed. "I would like that."

They joined the two men in the living room. Jennifer smiled for Scott's benefit as she joined him on the couch. The fact she had survived a trip to the nursery was her biggest accomplishment in weeks. She was very relieved to have the experience over, but also very glad she had agreed.

The evening ended shortly thereafter. It was late. Without anything being said, Scott knew his sister was tired. Frank was sent to the greenhouse to bring back two beautiful violets. Jennifer gracefully accepted the gift.

Goodbyes were said without being drawn out.

Jennifer leaned her head back against the seat as Scott pulled the car out of the drive. She let out her breath in a deep sigh of relief.

"Was it that hard?"

Jennifer didn't bother to soften her answer. "Yes."

Scott looked over at her, curious, wishing she would explain. Everything he had seen said Jennifer and Heather had hit it off, were already on the way to becoming friends. Jennifer's assessment did not match his observation. "Why was it hard?" Scott asked, feeling the need to push for an answer.

"She's pregnant," Jennifer finally replied.

"That's a problem?"

She nodded.

Scott looked over at Jennifer, needing answers. Her expression stopped his next question. She was seriously hurting. He reached over to grasp her hand. This is the issue Lord, isn't it? "Talk to me, Jennifer. What's going on?"

It was time to tell him. She abruptly changed the subject. "Could we go for a walk on the beach? Could you handle another late night?"

Her request surprised him. "Sure, if you would like to."

"Please."

Chapter Seven

Even with her coat on, Jennifer found the night air too cold to walk far, and her shoes weren't made for walking on sand. At Scott's suggestion, they went back to his place. He built a fire. With all the lights off, the living room took on a soft glow as the flames flickered around the logs, the only sound an occasional loud snap and sizzle as the sap in the wood burned.

He pulled her down on the sofa beside him and tucked her gently against him. Her head cradled against his shoulder, Jennifer watched the flames in silence for some time. She could feel Scott breathing, even hear his heartbeat. His arms around her waist were strong and solid. It felt so good to be near him. It felt safe.

"I lost a baby girl," Jennifer said softly into the silence.

She felt Scott's reaction. The sudden stillness as his breathing stopped. "When, Jennifer?"

He understood her pain. It was in his voice, in the way he was suddenly holding her. He understood her pain and was sharing it. Somewhere inside Jennifer a glimmer of hope began to form. She had taken such a risk in saying those words. Letting Scott see a memory that was still raw and unhealed. He could hurt her so badly with just a wrong word.

She was crying. She had been so afraid Scott would be angry that she had not told him earlier.

Scott looked down at the face of the most important woman who had ever been in his life and had to close his eyes at the pain he saw. His arms tightened around her. "Honey, it's okay. It's going to be okay." He was not able to think of anything else to say. He rocked her gently in his arms and let her cry. He felt a few tears slip down his own face as well. She had been holding the memory inside all this time. So much now made sense. Her anger at God. Her hesitancy to really talk with him. Scott groaned. Her reluctance to be around young children. How could he have missed seeing something so desperately wrong? She was a lady fighting a battle with grief so severe it had been crushing her heart and he had not understood. "Jennifer. Honey, it's going to be all right." He gently wiped away the tears streaming down her face. A baby. She would have made such a wonderful mother.

"Jennifer, tell me what happened." He needed to know. Please, Lord, help her to tell me.

There was a long silence as she tried to stop the tears. Scott waited, stroking her arms lightly, feeling the occasional tremor that ran down her back. She was in so much pain.

"I couldn't carry her to term. She was born badly premature." She let out a shaky breath. "She was so beautiful, Scott. So awful tiny. She only weighed two pounds, two ounces. Her feet were less than an inch long, her fingers couldn't even circle my little finger. She was less than eleven inches long. She was the most beautiful baby I had ever seen." She took a deep breath and let it out on a sob. "They said she wouldn't live. Her lungs were not developed, and the stress of having to breathe before she was physically ready to do so was such a crisis for her. But she was born, and alive, and she was going to live. You could see it in her blue eyes. She was such a fighter."

Scott gently brushed the hair back from Jennifer's face, watching her expression, the pain, seeing the incredible intensity of love she had felt for her daughter. He could feel the crushing pain inside his own heart at what was coming. God, why?

Jennifer smiled at a memory from the past. "But she did live, Scott. And she finally learned how to suck and she started to gain weight and she got stronger, and they even began to talk about miracles happening. I started to make her little clothes so she would have something to wear when she came home. I would spend my days at the hospital holding her and talking to her and telling her about her dad and she would smile at me with those vivid blue eyes."

There was a very long silence and Scott did not disturb it. He couldn't.

"She was ten weeks old when she got the cold. In the last week when she no longer had the energy to move, she would lie in the incubator and watch me with her vivid blue eyes and blink at me as I talked to her. She struggled so hard for each breath. I got my hand inside the incubator around all the tubes and slid my finger under her hand and stroked the back of her arm, and I prayed a very simple prayer. Lord, she needs another breath. And when she breathed, I would say thank you and I would pray again. We were a team. I prayed and God answered and she breathed."

The words stopped. A heavy shudder shook her frame. "At 10:02 p.m. on Wednesday, December 10, I prayed, and God didn't answer, and my baby didn't breathe."

Oh, God. How could You crush someone's faith so callously? Of all the ways the baby could have died, why did you destroy Jennifer's faith in the process? Scott had never felt such anger before in his entire life. Never at a person. Never at his God. But it erupted full blown as he heard what Jennifer said.

"What was her name, Jennifer? What was your daughter's name?"

"Colleen." She said it on a whisper. "Colleen Marie St. James."

He didn't often call his sister in the middle of the night, but Scott picked up the phone at 2:00 a.m. when he got back from taking Jennifer home and dialed Heather's number. He had to talk to someone. She answered the phone on the third ring. "Twig."

"What's wrong, Scott? Mom?" There was alarm in her voice.

"No, all the family is fine. I need to talk about Jennifer."

There was silence for a minute as she woke up and regrouped. "What's wrong, Scott?"

"I just found out Jennifer lost a baby girl, Twig." He drew a deep, shaky breath. "I was okay when she told me, now I feel like I'm falling apart. I don't know what to do. She's been bleeding inside with grief because she lost a daughter."

"Oh, Scott. If I'd only known. I spent the evening talking about my pregnancy, showing her the nursery."

"You didn't know. Neither of us did. I should have put the pieces together earlier." He took another deep breath, fighting to stop the tears that wanted to come from deep in his gut. "Jennifer was pregnant when Jerry died. Did her best to keep herself together for the baby's sake. But the strain was too much, Colleen was born over two months premature. She beat the odds and made it through the first few days, apparently began to improve rapidly, after two months there was talk of letting her go home. Then she got sick and took a turn for the worse. She was three months old when she died.

"Jennifer has been blaming herself for the child's death, that it was her fault the child was premature. She could barely talk tonight, she was hurting so much." He ran a hand through his hair. "I don't know how to help her, Twig."

"Give her time, Scott. At least she's grieving. That's better than denying the pain of what happened."

"Without meaning to, I could really hurt her right now. Should I talk about it now that I know? Try not to talk about it?"

"Does she have any family in the area?"

"Her brother and his wife. Jennifer seems close to both Peter and Rachel."

"Then let her set the pace, Scott. From what you said, she's been fairly open about her late husband."

"Yes."

"She'll reach the point she can talk about Colleen the same way. It will just take time."

"Thank you, Twig. I'm sorry I had to wake you up."

"That's okay, Scott. I'll pray for you both. You can handle this. Please, try not to worry tonight. Try to get some sleep."

"I'll try."

He put the phone down slowly after saying good-night. Time. His concept of how long he thought she needed had just been overtaken by a new reality. "Jennifer, I'll give you all the time you need. I promise you that," he whispered. "But I'm not going to let you retreat back into a shell now. Not after you have finally begun to face the pain. We'll get through this together. I'm not going to let you be alone in your grief anymore."

He lay awake for hours that night, fighting God over the senseless way Colleen had died, angry at the pain, angry at the brutal fact such a simple heartfelt prayer had not been answered. The anger did not change the circumstances, but he found in himself an intense willingness to go toe to toe with God to at least ensure Jennifer got an answer to the question of Why. She was going to be his wife. His God could not leave her like this. He had to at least heal the pain.

You've left her torn apart for three years, God. That makes no sense. I know You. You don't act this way. You don't rip apart and walk away. Why haven't You helped her? Why haven't You intervened? This isn't like You. You have to get back in this game and ease her pain. Is not one of Your names Comfort? I don't see love here, or comfort. Does it give You pleasure to leave her trapped in grief? How could You do this to the woman I love?

"Hi," Scott said quietly when she opened the door. He wished he had worn his sunglasses, taken more than the three aspirins, done something more to ease the pain radiating behind his eyes. He was at her door as early as he thought safe. He didn't want to have their first conversation be over a phone. He knew how the grief was going to hit her, and the last thing he wanted was distance between them when they talked. She looked awful but he didn't care. He felt as bad as she did.

"Hi," Jennifer replied softly, not meeting his eyes. She opened the door for him and Scott stepped inside. She felt very self-conscious this morning. She didn't know what to say after last night. She knew she looked a mess, and that didn't help any.

"I brought these for you." He took a ribbon-tied set of three roses from behind his back, one red, one peach, one white.

"Thank you, Scott," she said, fighting tears. Why did he have to be so nice? "They are beautiful."

Scott watched her as she carried the flowers into the living room and added them to the vase on the end table. He frowned. "Jennifer, did you sleep at all last night?"

She brushed away a tear as she wearily shook her head. "I thought I was over these crying jags months ago, Scott. Last night, every time I closed my eyes I was back in that hospital lounge, waiting for word about Colleen, or wearing that awful green gown I always had to wear when I was around her, trying to hold her despite all the machines around her"—she grimaced—"remembering what it was like when she died."

Scott crossed over to join her, his hands lightly touching her shoulders, turning her toward him. "Look at me, honey."

She finally did.

He hated the look in her eyes. They were dying again. "I am glad you told me. I know how hard it was. I'm angry with God for how Colleen died. She was your daughter, and you shouldn't have had to suffer the loss of both your husband and your daughter. But you have to deal with the grief and get beyond this, Jennifer. You've got no choice. You will have other children someday." It was the only thing promising that he had been able to find last night. She would have other children. God willing, they would be his. She was afraid of the idea right now, afraid of having more children, he knew it, he could feel it, but given time, her grief would eventually heal.

Jennifer didn't say anything. She blinked a couple of times, and he couldn't tell if she'd even heard him. She turned away to walk to the window, wearily rubbed the back of her neck, and he wondered how bad her headache was. "I'm sorry I didn't tell you sooner," she said. "Several times I have wanted to talk about her, but I could never find the right words."

The wall he had feared was up between them. He wasn't going to be getting close to her grief today. She had pushed it and the pain too far down to be touched. Scott closed his eyes and took a deep breath. Now was not the time to push. She desperately needed a break. The crisis the morning he had met her was nothing compared to the crisis that was coming, unless she got some help. She wasn't going to make it through this pain. She hadn't slept, and her emotions were becoming deadened. Mentally, physically, she didn't have the reserves to deal with what had happened. And if he wasn't careful, she was going to see his presence as adding to her pain. He knew about the prayer, he knew the details of her crisis of faith. And her brother, Peter, didn't. He had realized that sometime during the night. She had never told Peter and Rachel about praying for Colleen to breathe. It had remained her private battle with God. The fact he knew made him dangerous to her now. If he wasn't careful, she was going to push him away, just as she was trying to push away the pain.

In an insight that seemed to come directly from the Lord, he asked, "Would you like to go out on the lake for a couple of hours? It's promising to be a relatively warm, sunny day. We could even do a little fishing if you like. It's peaceful out on the water and you don't have to think about anything, just watch your bobber. It might help you sleep. The wind and water always have that effect on me."

She turned to look at him—the quiet, calm, studying look she'd given on the pier the morning she had come back to the beach. It was radiating out from the strength inside, reserves he'd seen her tap that very first morning when she'd been so tired it had been hard for her to walk a straight line. "You're taking the day off work?"

"I figured you might like some company."

It earned him a soft real smile. It disappeared too quickly, but it gave him hope. She crossed back to his side, squeezed his hand. "Thank you, Scott. I really appreciate that. Yes, let's go out on the lake for a bit. I like to fish. Should I pack us a lunch?"

"I'll pack a cooler with drinks to take along. If we catch anything, we can fix them for lunch. If not, there is a restaurant built out on the lake down at the harbor. We can eat there," Scott replied, improvising everything.

She seemed willing to let him. "I'll just get changed and be back in a minute."

Jennifer changed clothes, her movements heavy and forced. Her reserves were gone, she was weary beyond words. She had already decided she was going to lean on Scott to the literal extent he would allow her. She was tired of fighting God. Tired of caring. Tired of coping. Today she was going to leave all the misery here at the house and ignore it all for as long as she could. It had been such a long, painful night. There were no more tears to shed. She had ended up standing in the doorway to the room that had once been prepared as her daughter's nursery, and she had sobbed there until she'd thought her heart would break. But her heart had stayed intact, and the hours had passed, and she'd eventually, wearily, headed to the kitchen to fix coffee and toast as the sun rose.

They left the house, Scott carrying her windbreaker for

her, and he carefully made sure her seat belt was fastened once she was seated in the passenger seat. Jennifer leaned her head back against the headrest and closed her eyes and listened to the music Scott had turned on. She was almost dozing when they reached his house.

Jennifer looked over at Scott as they walked down to the pier together, her hand tucked firmly in his, and was incredibly grateful to no longer be alone. When she saw the boat she smiled. It had been designed for one specific thing, fishing, and the sight of it brought back ancient memories from her past, and she was glad she had come.

"Watch your step." Scott offered a hand to help her down into the boat.

The boat was designed to seat four. Jennifer moved forward to the middle seat.

Scott handed her a life jacket.

Once the cooler and the towels were stashed, Scott took his seat. He slipped the key into the ignition. The outboard motor started instantly. Leaving the motor idling, he got up to untie the mooring lines. "I'll run us over to the Harbor Stop to fill up the gas tank, get bait, then we'll head out to Westminster Bridge."

Jennifer nodded.

Once they cleared the No Wake zone, Scott opened the motor up, giving enough speed to lift the bow out of the water. Jennifer deliberately left last night at the pier and forced herself into beginning to relax. And unexpectedly she found her spirits beginning to lift as the bright sun and sky replaced her sense of darkness with the vividness of a beautiful day.

After close to five minutes of running, they passed Courtline Point and were out on the open water. The wind picked up.

Jennifer swiveled around to face Scott.

"Do you need me to slow down?"

Jennifer shook her head. "You're fine. The spray is cold even with the jacket."

"We'll be at The Harbor Stop in another four to five minutes."

Scott cut the speed down to comply with the No Wake rule as they entered the protected cove. Jennifer turned back to the front, impatiently brushing her hands through her hair to get it out of her eyes. She should have tied it back before she left. It was going to take twenty minutes with a brush to get her hair untangled.

The Harbor Stop turned out to be a supply store built out on the water, floating on pontoons at the lake level. A series of docks had slips to hold fifty boats. Scott piloted the boat to the east side of the store so he could moor within reach of the gas pumps. Intent on watching his distance, Scott didn't realize Jennifer had the forward mooring line in her hands, until, as the boat touched the dock with a gentle bump, she flipped the line over the tie point and brought the boat in snug to the dock. "Okay, Scott, you can cut the engine." She gave the line four figure-eights around the north-south prongs of the tie point, adding an extra turn to each loop. The line would not slip.

"Thanks."

"Sure." She looked around the boat. "Do you have a bait bucket for the minnows?"

"Behind you on the left. It's in the live well." Scott replied. He stepped out of the boat onto the dock. He had missed something. The bow moor line she had tied was a duplicate of the stern line he had tied. Jennifer was not a novice to boats.

Scott took the minnow bucket and offered her a hand out of the boat. She took his hand without hesitation. "Thanks."

Following Scott's example she dropped her life jacket back on her seat. "Gas first or bait?"

"Bait," Scott decided.

Leaving Scott to get the minnows, Jennifer wandered around to check out the store. There was a collection of paperbacks on the back wall. She paged through a mystery she recognized.

"Jennifer."

She turned, surprised to find Scott beside her.

"Try these on." He was holding a pair of sunglasses.

"Scott, I don't need—"

He cut her off with a smile. "Try them on."

Jennifer tried them on.

"What do you think? Do they fit all right?"

She smiled. "You made a good choice, Scott. They fit fine."

"Good."

He took the glasses. "Do me a favor and see if they have any chocolate cookies."

Jennifer laughed. "Okay." Her hands gently pushed his chest. "You're suppose to be buying the bait, Scott."

"Okay, okay."

Ten minutes later, Scott offered Jennifer a hand back into the boat.

"How far is Westminster Bridge?"

"About ten minutes west of here," he replied, stowing the minnow bucket where it would not shift. Jennifer clipped on her life jacket. She leaned forward to untie the bow moor line.

Scott started the engine. "Okay, Jennifer."

She released the line and pushed them away from the dock. Once they cleared the No Wake zone, he opened the motor up, sending the boat skimming across the open water. Jennifer slipped on her new sunglasses. It had been a long time since she had spent a day on the water. She was determined to enjoy this.

The lake was long, constantly branching, with a multitude of coves and inlets. Scott eventually turned into one of the side branches of the lake. The inlet was over three hundred feet wide at the opening, narrowing as it went back. Westminster Bridge was a railroad crossing, the concrete pillars farther down the inlet. "We'll start in on this side and make the half circle of the inlet," Scott explained, slowing the engine as he took the boat in toward the shoreline.

Jennifer nodded. There were fallen trees in the water beneath them, their massive root structures visible on the bank and the trees angling out into the water. The banks, however, appeared to drop off very quickly; there was no evidence to suggest they were actually floating over old trees the lake had swallowed up.

Scott dropped anchor once they were about fifteen feet from the shore. Jennifer slipped off her life jacket, draping it across the seat in front of her. Scott tossed his life jacket up front beside hers. Finding the right key, he unlocked the storage compartment where the tackle was stored. There were a dozen different rods, different makes, different reels. "Take your pick, Jennifer," he offered.

"The blue one with the open-face reel."

Scott lifted the rod out for her. He brought out the gray rod and open-face reel for himself, his birthday present from his dad.

Jennifer took a look at the rod. It had a swivel, hook and weight already. All she needed was a bobber. "Can you reach the tackle box?"

He passed it forward.

"Thanks." Humming softly, Jennifer found what she

needed. Looping the line around the bobber, she slipped the metal spring back over the line to hold it in place.

She swiveled around to reach the minnow bucket. Jennifer closed her hand around one of larger ones. Smooth and slippery, it struggled to get free. She slipped the hook through the minnow's back behind its front fin. Studying the shoreline for a moment, she shifted around. Her cast sent the minnow and the bobber out parallel to the shore.

Watching her, Scott nodded his approval. She was not a novice at this by any means. She would get the best coverage of the territory by going parallel to the shore, rather than toward the shore. With a smile, Scott sent his line sailing out the other direction.

They followed the south bank, making their way toward the concrete pillars of Westminster Bridge. Scott was pleased to see the strain from last night beginning to fade from Jennifer's eyes. She was a born fisherman. She had a good eye for the water, a smooth cast, patience. She was clearly enjoying herself. She was also beating him hands down in terms of success. She had caught four bass, three of which were large enough to keep and dress.

Scott was enjoying watching her.

He needed to do something tangible to help her deal with her grief. It was the trauma of the loss that was so devastating. It was how Colleen had been born, how she had died that was the real problem he had to help Jennifer overcome. *Trauma.* The word kept coming back in his mind as he prayed. Jennifer was still caught by the event. When she had described those last few days when Colleen had fought for each breath, Scott had been able to see her there, sitting beside the incubator with her hand reaching inside and holding Colleen's, praying for each breath Colleen needed to take. He could see the shock that would have crossed her face when her last prayer for breath had not been answered. Colleen had died.

Trauma.

Scott couldn't comprehend the shock of what it must have been like to have such a simple prayer not answered. Jennifer had fallen so deeply in love with Colleen. It was in her voice, her face, her emotions. To watch her daughter die... Scott shook his head, flinching inside at the pain the image created.

How could he take Jennifer out of the place she was in now to a place where the trauma could lessen? Maybe it was happening already. The movie theater and the shock he had observed. The long night of tears last night. She was finally coming alive and feeling the pain and the grief and facing the trauma. And she had worked up the courage to tell him. They all had to be steps in the right direction.

He was furious at God for having put them in this situation. It was going to take more than one day for his own emotions to accept what had happened. He'd find a way. She needed him to be past the anger. But she had been working against the anger for almost three years, he'd been feeling it less than twenty-four hours. He needed time and answers, too.

They reached the bridge. Scott used the trolling motor to take them out away from shore and back into the main waterway. He cut the engine when they were some twenty feet from the base of the pillars; they would drift in closer. "I've had some luck around the base of the pillars," he offered. "It's deep here, around thirty feet."

Jennifer nodded. She cast her line out toward the first concrete pillar.

Scott watched her for a moment, before leaning forward to reach the minnow bucket and bait his own line. He cast his line out toward the second pillar. The bait dropped into the water a few inches from the concrete pillar. The bait had no more than hit the water then his bobber was gone.

Jennifer smiled. "You weren't kidding." She turned to watch him bring the fish in. The rod bowed down a foot as the line strained. The fish was trying to go deep. Scott turned him back.

"Nice fish." Jennifer commented as Scott brought him in over the side. It was a good-size crappie. Catching Scott's line, she slid her hand down to grasp the top of the hook and hold the fish still. Sliding her hand down the body of the fish, she lowered the back fins so she would not get spiked. He was almost too large for her hand. The hook came out easily, he'd been snagged through the side of his mouth.

Jennifer swiveled around so she could measure the fish. "Ten and three-quarter inches. Not bad."

Scott smiled. "He'll dress nicely," he agreed. He opened up the live well and Jennifer released the crappie in with the three bass she had caught earlier.

Jennifer leaned over the side of the boat to wash off her hands. Scott tossed her the towel. "Thanks." She wiped her hands and draped the towel across the seat.

The next fish went to Jennifer. It was a sunfish, which surprised her, given the size of the hook she was using. She leaned over the side of the boat and released it gently. She looked up to find Scott watching her. "What?" she asked, confused by his look.

"You've got a soft heart."

"Only for babies," she replied, but her smile was beautiful.

They fished along the pillars for a while, then moved to the north bank, slowly propelled by the trolling motor. Jennifer had not said anything, but Scott could tell she was getting to the end of her energy reserves. They had been out almost three hours. He was ready to suggest they head in when her bobber dropped below the surface with a jerk as the minnow four feet below the surface was hit.

She had a fighter. Scott pulled in his line to give her room to maneuver. Twice the fish turned in to the boat, then ran out again, forcing Jennifer to give up line or risk losing him.

The bass broke the surface on its third turn.

"Wow."

"He's a trophy, Jennifer." Scott hoped her line would hold.

Jennifer brought the fish to the side of the boat on the fifth turn. Scott got underneath him with the net and brought the bass over the side of the boat. The largemouth bass slapped angrily against the confinement. Scott took a firm grip on his lower lip. "Okay, Jennifer."

She slid the net free. "How's he hooked?"

"It's down in the side of his mouth."

Jennifer dug out the needle-nose pliers. "At least he didn't swallow it."

Scott held the fish firmly as Jennifer went after the hook. "Can you reach it?"

She got a firm grip on the eye of the hook, pushed it down. "Got it." She brought the hook out.

"Take him firmly by the bottom lip and put him against the tape, Jennifer. Let's find out how big he really is." Scott handed her back her prize fish.

He was heavy, cold. Jennifer laid him against the measuring tape on the side of the boat. "Twenty-one and a quarter inches," she finally decided. "He's the second largest bass I've ever caught." He was a beautiful fish.

"Would you like to have him mounted?"

Jennifer looked at the fish in her hands. "No. This one gets to go free." Leaning over the side, she lowered the fish down into the water. For a brief moment he remained motionless in her hands, able to swim free, but choosing not to move. Then he was gone with a slap against her hand.

Scott handed her a dry towel. "What's your record?"

"Twenty-six and a half inches. I caught him down on Lake Tahoe eight years ago," she replied.

"You've certainly got another story to tell with this one."

"You can say that again. He was beautiful."

"I think that one is going to be impossible to top. Shall we head in?"

Jennifer looked regretfully at the water, but had to concede she was exhausted. "Yes."

Scott nodded and moved back to his seat. Jennifer quietly began storing their gear in the lockers. She handed Scott his life jacket, then slipped on her own.

"Ready?"

She nodded.

"Where's the best place to clean the fish?" she asked as the boat pulled up to his pier.

"I have a cleaning table already set up in the boathouse. I can handle this part of it, Jennifer, if you would like to go ahead and take the cooler up to the house." He handed her the keys.

"Anything you need?"

"A pan of water to put the fish in. Try the cupboard to the left of the sink."

"No problem. I'll be right back."

Scott had already cleaned two crappie by the time Jennifer joined him. She set down the pan of water on the worktable beside him. "Thanks."

Jennifer watched him fillet the first bass. His movements were smooth. She could appreciate the skill. Jennifer quietly studied him as he worked.

Scott looked over, caught her look. He smiled. "For lunch,

how about if we wrap the fish in foil with a little garlic butter and almonds, put it over a hot grill? Maybe fix baked potatoes, as well? There is fruit salad in the refrigerator," Scott
suggested as he worked.

"Sounds wonderful," Jennifer agreed. She smiled. "I just
realized how hungry I am."

Scott chuckled. "Nothing is better than fresh fish when
you are hungry." Their footsteps echoed across the red-
wood deck.

It had been a long time since she had done such a normal
thing as setting the table, Jennifer realized as she set their
places. It was odd, how being a widow changed things. It
wasn't worth the effort to fix a meal for one, so she rarely
had a need to sit at her dining room table. More often than
not, she ate a sandwich at her desk while she worked. She
had missed this normal routine.

She joined Scott on the patio when she had finished. "The
coals should be ready in about fifteen minutes," he commented, adjusting the vents under the grill. He accepted the
cold soda she had brought him. "To save time, I think we'll
bake the potatoes in the microwave. I'm ready to eat."

Jennifer chuckled. "No debate here."

It proved to be a very simple recipe for fixing the fish. A
piece of foil, several pats of butter, a little lemon juice, a
dusting of garlic and lots of sliced almonds. The foil was
twisted into a thin tube. "Nice," Jennifer commented.

Scott smiled. "Simple. I eat a lot of fresh fish."

Jennifer was pulling the hot potatoes from the microwave
when Scott pushed shut the patio door, carrying a platter
of fresh baked fish. "That smell's wonderful."

Scott set the platter down on the hot pad Jennifer had
found for the table. "Wait till you taste it, Jennifer. It's un-
believably good." He held her chair out for her. "Be care-

ful when you open the foil, there will be a lot of steam," he cautioned.

Jennifer savored her first bite. "This is delicious."

Scott smiled.

They talked casually over lunch, both avoiding talking about last night. Jennifer finished off two full packets of the fish, as well as the baked potato, before admitting she was full. The fruit salad made a delicious dessert. "That was a great meal." She stifled a yawn as she finished the sentence.

Scott debated offering her coffee, but the whole point of the day had been to help her sleep. If he took her home now she would probably fall asleep in the car, and that was not a very comfortable place to get some rest. "I have a lot of guest rooms here, Jen. Why don't you take a short nap and then I'll run you home. I have a couple of calls to return." The answering machine had been blinking when he checked it before lunch, but none of the calls had been urgent.

"Scott..."

"Please."

"A guest room would be very welcome."

He offered her a hand. "Come on, I'll show you upstairs." Jennifer let him escort her down the hall and to the stairway.

This was not a smart move. Jennifer was trying to form the words to back out and ask him to take her straight home, but they had reached the top of the stairs before she could get the words in order. Scott stopped by the first door. "Here you go." It was a beautiful bedroom. Delicate rose print wallpaper. Thick cream carpet. The dressers, the bookshelf, the bed, all early American antiques. A colorful homemade wedding ring quilt was folded neatly at the foot of the bed.

She looked lost. Scott forced himself to smile gently, leave her there. "I'll be in my office if you need me. Just turn right at the bottom of the stairs. You can't miss it."

"Thanks, Scott," she said faintly.

He closed the door softly behind him as he left.

Jennifer stood inside the door of the room for some time, getting used to the sounds of a foreign place, letting her nerves settle. She should not be here. She sighed. She was in no shape to leave. She moved hesitantly toward the bed. Scott was right, she needed to sleep.

She sat down on the edge of the bed. It was a nice mattress, not too soft, nor too hard. She slipped off her shoes. After a few minutes more thinking about it, she turned the covers down and stretched out. Immediately her body relaxed. Her sleep was that of exhaustion.

Chapter Eight

Scott quietly pushed the door of the guest room open. It was a little over an hour since he had shown Jennifer to the guest room. She was asleep, as he'd hoped. She had one hand tucked under the pillow, one hand curled under her chin. Her wedding ring was leaving a mark on her face. Scott carefully shifted her hand. He studied her for a few more moments before quietly slipping out of the room.

The grandfather clock in the downstairs hallway was chiming six-thirty as Scott again quietly pushed open the guest room door. She had not stirred in hours. Scott set a single rose down on the bedside table and tucked a note under the stem. Frowning slightly, he paused by her bedside. She was exhausted. But if she slept much longer she would not be able to sleep tonight.

"Jennifer." He gently shook her shoulder. "Jen, it's time to wake up."

"Go away, Jerry," she murmured, rolling over and taking the quilt with her.

He chuckled. "Jen, it's Scott. Come on, honey, wake up."

Her face appeared from beneath the quilt. She blinked at him a couple of times, then groaned. "How long have I been asleep?"

"About four hours," Scott replied.

She rubbed her eyes with the back of her hands. "I'm sorry, Scott. I could have slept at my own place."

He grinned. "No problem. I like having you here. I laid out fresh towels and a new toothbrush in the guest bathroom if you would like to freshen up. Dinner is in twenty minutes." He turned toward the door.

"Scott." He paused by the door and turned to look back. She ran her hand through her hair. "I need to go home. I can't impose on you any longer."

He just smiled. "Nonsense. Twenty minutes." He disappeared out the door.

Jennifer pushed back the quilt and sat on the edge of the bed. There was a single peach rosebud on the end table. "Oh, Scott. It's beautiful." She picked up the rose, gently fingering the soft petals. The note lying under the rose was clearly meant for her. She picked it up. "Jen, stay for dinner. Please. Scott."

The note folded in her hand. "Okay, Scott," Jennifer whispered quietly. She pushed herself to her feet. Her legs tottered beneath her. "Come on, Jennifer, wake up," she chided herself.

She found the towels and the toothbrush laid out on the bathroom counter just as Scott had described. Back in the guest bedroom five minutes later, her face washed and her unruly hair pulled back into place, Jennifer quickly straightened the covers on the bed.

Carrying her shoes, Jennifer went downstairs. She dropped the shoes on the rug by the front door. Scott was in the kitchen, humming a tune along with the radio as he tossed a large salad. "Something smells delicious," Jennifer remarked, pausing in the doorway as she took in the scene.

Scott looked up. He smiled. "Lasagna." Wiping his hands on a towel, he came over to join her. She looked so much better. Her eyes were clear, she had color back in her face.

"How are you feeling?"

"Not bad," Jennifer replied. "A little groggy."

They sat down to dinner a few minutes later.

He was in love with this lady. Scott didn't fight the growing conviction in his heart. Having her here made his house feel like a home. He'd give a lot to make this a permanent arrangement.

"Did your calls go well?"

"Yes. Most were just clarification."

She nodded. "What did you do while I slept all afternoon?"

I spent the afternoon thinking about asking you to marry me. He didn't say the words. She was not ready for that discussion. She wouldn't be until she dealt with what she had lost. Her husband. Her daughter. But the day was coming when she would be ready. He was an optimistic man; someday she was going to be ready to get married and have a family again. He answered her question about his afternoon. "I worked on making a dog bed. Heather and Frank have offered me a choice from Blackie's latest litter."

Jennifer nodded. "Quigley is adorable."

"Thanks. I thought so."

They had finished dinner. "Interested in some coffee?"

Jennifer nodded. "Sounds good," she agreed.

They cleared the table together.

"Let's take the coffee into the library," Scott suggested.

He led the way through the quiet house. Scott pushed open the French doors across from the living room. "This is the library, and beyond it, my office."

It was a small room, formal, with a love seat and two chairs, two antique mahogany tables. The four walls were recessed bookshelves. She could spend hours enjoyably browsing this room. She idly walked along the shelves, reading titles.

"Your books are on the third shelf to your left."

Jennifer looked over. She smiled. "They look impressive, all lined up together."

Scott smiled. "They certainly do."

Jennifer sat on the love seat. Scott chose the seat across from her, stretched out his legs.

"I love this room, Scott."

"I thought you might," Scott replied. "I'm glad you agreed to come today."

"I've enjoyed it," Jennifer agreed. She sipped carefully on the hot coffee. It was delicious.

"It's chocolate mocha," Scott said, noticing her surprise.

"I like it."

"Jennifer, would you come to church with me this weekend?"

She didn't answer for some time. "I might," she replied. "Why are you asking?"

"You need to heal that relationship, Jen, or you are not going to be able to put this behind you."

"Scott, you can't fix things just because you want them to be different. My daughter died. God was the only one who could intervene. He didn't. That is not easy to move beyond. I feel like I was betrayed."

"Have you told Him that?"

"Yes."

"What has He said in reply?"

She didn't say anything for some time. "I haven't listened to find out."

"Are you at the point where you can listen?"

"Maybe." She had to admit she would like her relationship with God healed. "If I go to church with you, people will think we're a couple."

Exactly. "I'll do my best not to put you in any uncomfortable position."

She nodded. "I'll go with you."

"Thank you."

She smiled slightly. "I don't sing very well. Just to warn you."

"I won't hold it against you." She looked very peaceful sitting there, her feet tucked beneath her, her head resting back against the couch. He was beginning to recognize the expressions on her face. She was thinking about the past again.

"I wish I had a picture of Colleen with me so I could show it to you. She had such vivid blue eyes. She used to tilt her head just this certain way and look at you. Then smile.

"She was so tiny when she was born it was a struggle for her to be awake. It took all her energy. So she would lie there and blink at me with this surprised expression in her eyes. They had to feed her through patches on her back for the first two weeks. It was such a wonderful day when she began to suck."

"What do you miss the most, Jennifer?"

"The fact my life doesn't revolve around her anymore. She gave me a reason to get up every morning. Even if the routine consisted of going to the hospital for the day and sitting with her, she was there. It was devastating after she died not to have her there. I had grown so attached."

"Do you think about having other children?"

"No, never. Colleen was such a traumatic experience, it is going to take a long time for the intensity of those memories to fade. I couldn't risk going through that again."

"You loved Colleen. You would love another child with the same intensity."

"In my mind will always be the fact I lost my eldest daughter."

She opened her eyes to look over at him. "Scott, you don't watch someone you love die without carrying that image with you forever. There isn't room inside me to love another child, the grief for Colleen is too large. It shadows everything I have done in the past three years."

Scott wished he could ease the pain she felt. "Have you ever considered writing about Colleen?"

Jennifer just shook her head in reply and then sipped her coffee.

The room was silent for several minutes.

"Why haven't you ever married? You're not a bachelor at heart."

He smiled slightly. "I don't know. I've never met anyone I wanted to spend the rest of my life with."

"Are you close to your parents?"

"Yes. We have always been a close family. It's been that way for several generations."

"You have a large extended family?"

"I have five cousins, most with families, and my grand-parents on my mother's side are still alive. What about you? Is it just you and Peter?"

"Yes."

He could not comprehend being that alone. It was a dreadful thought.

It was hard to let the evening end on such a heavy note.

But he didn't try to lighten it. Jennifer needed the time to just have someone listen.

"I guess I'd better get going now." Jennifer set her mug down on the coffee table. Scott glanced at his watch and agreed that it was getting late.

They drove to Jennifer's house in a comfortable silence. She hugged him when they said good-night. "Thank you for today, Scott. I needed it."

"I'm glad I was able to help." He gently brushed her cheek with his hand. "Try to sleep, okay?"

She nodded. "Good night, Scott."

Chapter Nine

There was a good crowd at the Sunday morning services. Jennifer smoothed down her floral dress nervously as she got out of the car.

"You look beautiful, Jennifer."

She barely heard the compliment she was so nervous. "You said Frank and Heather will be here?"

Scott nodded. "Frank is teaching Sunday school this morning, so only Heather will be in the services." He caught hold of her hand, carried their Bibles in his other hand. "If you would prefer not to sit with Heather, I can ensure they never even know we are here."

"No. I would like to sit with someone I know. Scott, I hate these first times. All your friends are going to wonder who I am."

He smiled. "Let them wonder. We'll slip in and out before they can come over to be introduced."

"No. If you do that they will really start to speculate about who you were with."

He laughed. "Relax, Jen. They are nice people. They will like you. Would it be so bad for them to know we are friends?"

"I guess not." He opened the front glass door for them. "But I hate this," she whispered to him.

He hugged her waist. "Do you want to be introduced as Jennifer or Mrs. St. James?" he whispered back.

"Jennifer. Wait—no. Someone might take my wedding ring to be an engagement ring."

"If they do, we'll just say it's true," he teased.

"Scott."

"Spoilsport." It got him the smile he'd been trying to coax out of her.

They had reached the auditorium. Scott guided Jennifer toward the left section. "Good morning, Twig."

"Hi, Scott. Jennifer, I'm glad you could come." Heather's smile was genuine, and Jennifer realized she was also nervous. Scott had called his sister and told her they were coming, that was obvious. Jennifer slid into the pew to sit beside Heather.

"Jennifer, this is for you." Heather handed her a card. "I was so sorry to hear about Colleen."

"Heather, thank you," Jennifer replied, surprised. "You didn't have to do this."

"I felt so awful about Thursday night. I couldn't have been more insensitive."

"You didn't know."

"I should have been more observant, I'm so very sorry."

Jennifer opened the card and read it, had to fight not to cry. She had promised herself she would not cry today. "Heather, it's a perfect card. Thank you."

The services started. Jennifer felt herself pulled into the music. It felt good to be standing beside Scott sharing a hymn book with him. Not being in a position where others saw her and felt sad for her. It was one of the reasons she had stopped going to church with Peter and Rachel. It had been the church she and Jerry attended, and after he had died, she had simply not been able to deal with the pity.

Scott had a good voice.

It had been too long since she'd been in church. As the service progressed, Jennifer just tried to absorb it all. The choir was singing softly as the communion was passed.

As open as he was with her, the man seated beside her, deep in prayer, was a mystery to her. Scott had needed this morning she realized as she watched him searching out and finding God. This was where he got the strength to walk through his difficult weeks. Jennifer swallowed hard.

God, I'm sorry I have been fighting you so much. I know with absolute certainty that You did hear that prayer for breath. I don't understand why You answered it by saying no. Please help me accept what happened and go on, to accept the fact there will be no explanations for me to find. Only You. I still wonder if I prayed something wrong that time, if it was something I did that resulted in that specific prayer not being answered when the hundred prayers before that were answered. I'm still so angry, Lord. I'm trying to let that pain and anger go, but it's hard to the point of being impossible. When I see You face-to-face, I will understand why it had to be this way. Please, until that day, will You give me the grace to accept what happened and move on? I need you, Lord.

Heather was the one who silently slipped her tissues. Jennifer accepted them gratefully. All she seemed to do this past month was cry.

Scott gripped her hand. Jennifer wanted to lay her head against his shoulder and ask for a hug that would never end. Some things would have to remain a wish.

The sermon was good, but Jennifer remembered little of it.

When the service was over, neither Heather nor Scott questioned her earlier tears. They seemed to have a plan already worked out between them. Heather was the one doing all the introductions as they met friends. Jennifer was aware of the speculation going on. Scott had never dropped her hand. The people she met seemed very nice.

They walked out to the parking lot together. Scott was so proud of her. It had felt so right having her beside him. He longed for the day that would be permanent. He wished they could spend the day together again, but he didn't want to pressure her.

"That wasn't too bad was it?" Scott asked as they drove to her home.

"No. I liked your church."

"I hoped you would."

He walked her to her door a few minutes later. He gently dropped his arms around her shoulders and pulled her into a hug. "Thank you," he said softly, brushing back the hair from her face. "It meant a lot to me that you came."

She hugged him back. "It helped."

"I'm glad." He hesitated before letting her go. "I'll call you," he said, stepping away, smiling.

She smiled back. "Okay."

Jennifer wandered around her house for almost an hour, cleaning things that were already clean, straightening things that looked fine. *"Have you ever thought about writing about Colleen?"* The words Scott had said Friday were haunting her. She picked up a pad of paper and went to stretch out on her bed. "If I were to write about Colleen, what would I want to say?" She wrote the question down on the top of the page. The tears began to come. "That I loved my daughter."

It was a soul-cleansing four hours. When she got up from the bed, her neck and shoulders were stiff, her eyes were sore, her hand tense from writing. But the raw pain was gone from her heart. It was on paper now. It was something that could be touched and shared and thought about. She set the pad of paper down on the nightstand and pulled down the comforter. Her feet were cold, there was a mountain of tissues tossed over the side of the bed, her eyes burned, and she desperately needed to sleep. But she felt better inside than she had in the past three years.

God, I can feel your peace inside for the first time in years. A safeness that feels like your arms wrapped tightly around me. Thank you for today. For all of it, the trepidation of going to services with Scott, the music, the sermon and the chance to begin healing by writing about Colleen. Please don't let this flicker of faith die. I know I've got such a long recovery still ahead of me.

She drifted to sleep with the light still on.

The phone was ringing, shrill and nearby and not stopping. It roused her groggily back to consciousness. "Hello?"

"Jennifer, I'm sorry. I didn't mean to wake you up."

She yawned and her jaw cracked. "It's okay, Scott." She rubbed her eyes and blinked hard trying to bring her clock into focus. "What time is it?"

"Seven-fifteen."

Did he mean evening or morning? She had no idea. "I was taking a nap. I didn't plan to sleep away the day."

"Andrew and I were just talking. I'm going to have to be

out of town for most of this week. I need to visit two clients in Denver."

Jennifer forced herself not to feel the disappointment that churned inside. She wanted to discuss with him what she had been thinking about. "I'll miss you," she finally said, willing to admit the obvious.

"It's mutual," Scott replied, and she smiled at the frustration she heard in his voice. "I would give anything to get out of this trip. I don't want to be miles away from you. Would you like to go out to dinner Saturday night when I get back?"

"Sure."

"Thank you." She heard the relief in his voice. "I am sorry I woke you up. I know you need the rest. I'll give you a call from Denver."

"I would like that."

"Probably every night."

She grinned. Was this good or bad? She wasn't sure. But it felt good. "I'll be waiting for your calls," she replied with a smile.

They said goodbye, and Jennifer hung up the phone and looked at the ceiling and smiled as she groaned. "God, it was bad enough to be going on a date again. Why did You send a guy who wants to get serious? Are You sure I'm ready for this?"

"You went to church with him Sunday," Rachel said, sliding into the seat across from Jennifer at the kitchen table. Jennifer nodded as she took another bite of the bacon, lettuce and peanut butter sandwich. She had passed on the tomatoes. They had talked about church repeatedly since Jennifer had made the decision to stop attending with Peter and Rachel. Rachel understood her reasons—having attended the church with Jerry, having had a baby shower for

Colleen there, having buried both Jerry and Colleen in that church—Jennifer simply found it too painful a place to be. She hated the pity in people's faces and constantly feeling like a widow. Rachel had offered to go with her to check out other churches in the area, but Jennifer had kept saying not yet, not willing to admit she was too angry at God to feel like going to church. Time had drifted by.

"I'm glad you went," Rachel said.

"So was I," Jennifer replied. "It helped, no one knowing about Jerry and Colleen. Has Karen forgiven me yet?"

Rachel smiled. "I think so. She makes a point of asking about you every week."

Karen had been a good friend at church, but her daughter had been born two weeks after Colleen, and Jennifer felt it necessary to keep her at a distance now. "I wish she understood it's nothing personal."

"She understands, Jen," Rachel said, passing her the bowl of fruit salad. "You'll go out with him again next week?"

Jennifer nodded.

It was tough to plot a story when it came from real life. Jennifer tossed the pad of paper back on the round table and got to her feet. Ann had the final draft of the last Thomas Bradford book. Jennifer was trying her best to figure out what she would write next. Abandoning her office, Jennifer picked up a novel she was reading and walked out to the backyard.

She settled into the hammock and stared up at the blue sky and white puffy clouds. She and Jerry had both loved this hammock as a place to think.

Scott's suggestion that she write about Colleen was creating a real dilemma. Part of her wanted to accept the challenge. She wanted to share her love for Colleen with her readers. She just couldn't come up with a story line that would intrigue them. Her own story—a couple in love decides to start a family, gets pregnant, the husband dies; the baby, born early, also dies—wasn't an interesting story. It was emotional, but it missed a plot line.

She should abandon this idea and get to work on a mystery. She knew how to write mysteries.

Could she take her story and make it a mystery? The thought made her begin to toss the book she held up in the air and catch it, toss it up again.

The mysteries she liked to write had a detective. Maybe the husband was a detective? She rejected that idea. The man would die halfway through the book—hard to write a story around him. Maybe the husband didn't die of natural causes. Maybe the detective was trying to solve the case—the wife and the baby were an interesting complication to a straightforward mystery.

No. The detective thinks the wife is a suspect, he's pressing her for information, and she goes into early labor. When the baby dies, the detective is going to feel personally responsible. Jennifer missed catching the book, and it fell to the ground.

He couldn't be directly responsible. Maybe he's a cop and his partner wants to push for information, she's the prime suspect, and he's holding his partner back as long as he can from directly questioning her, but they reach the point they have to bring her in and she then goes into early labor. The detective falls in love with this premature little girl.

To even out the reader's sympathies, it's going to turn out the lady had actually, unwittingly, played a part in her husband's murder. When the baby dies, she confesses what had really happened. The final scene is the detective at the graveside of the baby.

Jennifer tumbled out of the hammock and headed for her office.

Jennifer wasn't going to answer. Scott held the phone and listened to it ring. It was after ten o'clock. Where was she? It was too early for her to have turned in for the night. He'd been calling her at ten o'clock every night and normally she was there on the first ring. He was about ready to hang up after six rings when the phone was suddenly answered. "Hello?"

"Jen, hi," he couldn't keep the relief from his voice.

"Scott." He could hear her smile. "How are you? How's Denver today?" She was certainly not getting ready for bed. He'd never heard her this alive before. She sounded like she had been very busy.

"Denver is fine. We've about concluded the negotiations for a new contract with one of our key customers. What about you?"

She laughed. "I've just about got the entire plot line for my next book sketched out."

"Really? That's great. What's it about?"

"It's another mystery. In fact, I think I've got another series. The key person is a cop. He's a detective in homicide. He's got a partner who is proving to be a great secondary character—sarcastic and cynical, great with one-liners. I'm going to have each book in the series focus on a specific case they are trying to solve." Jennifer settled back in the recliner. She was in her office, had been working on a pad of paper filling in the plot sequence for the book when Scott had called. She intentionally did not go into the details of the first case she was going to have the detectives solve. "Could you help me with a name? I haven't found one I like."

"What do you know about him?"

"He's thirty-nine. Five foot ten. Divorced. Plays basketball. A good character. Solid ethics. Honest. Tough, but can be compassionate. Slightly jaded by what he has seen people do to one another."

Scott thought for a few minutes. "Granite Parks."

Jennifer was shocked. It was perfect. "How did you do that? I've been wrestling with his name for days! It's perfect."

Scott laughed. "Beginner's luck. Anything else you need?"

She smiled. "Your company. I miss you," she replied, meaning it. "When is your flight back?"

Her reply had pleased him, she could hear it in his voice. "Mid-morning, Saturday. I'll pick you up at seven for dinner?"

"I'm looking forward to it."

It was storming Saturday when Scott arrived to pick up Jennifer. A crashing storm that came with heavy rain, wind and severe lightning. He pulled into her drive and hurried to the shelter of the porch.

"Hi, Jennifer." Lightning cracked as she opened the front door, and he saw her flinch. He stepped inside and quickly closed the door. She was dressed in a soft dove gray dress with a red sash and her hair pulled back by a matching red bow. She looked gorgeous. And slightly frightened. He slipped off his wet jacket and pulled her into a hug. "Okay?"

Her head buried in his shoulder, she nodded. Another bolt of lightning lit up the living room, and she flinched. "I don't like lightning." Her perfume smelled like lilacs.

"This storm is passing," he said gently. "Give it another twenty minutes and I doubt it will even be raining." He gently rubbed her back. "I really missed you," he said lightly.

She gave him a hug. "I missed you, too." She stepped back and picked up his jacket. "Could we wait till this passes before we leave?"

"Sure."

Jennifer put his jacket across one of the kitchen chairs and they went into the living room. Scott chose to sit in the easy chair instead of beside her on the couch. He would like nothing better than to kiss her, but he was not going to do so. At least not until this night was over. He smiled at the thought and forced himself away from the subject. "How is the book progressing?" he asked.

Her face lit up. "I love this period of writing a book. I don't have to worry about the details and the choice of words or the length of the scenes. I've just been sitting down and writing. I've made an enormous amount of progress. I love Granite. He is the perfect character. He is as clear in my mind as Thomas Bradford."

"I'm glad. I've been worried about how well you could make this transition. You've been writing about Thomas Bradford for years."

"I was comfortable, and I think that was becoming a problem. Great stories come from taking risks. This story feels more alive, more dramatic."

"Do you have any idea how long it will take to write?"

"At least six months. It will be significantly longer than my other books. How did Denver turn out?"

Scott told her about the people he had met, the places they had gone to eat, what the flight back had been like. The storm was beginning to drift west. The lightning had ended and there was simply a light rain falling when they eventually left for the restaurant. Scott had chosen a small Chinese restaurant that not many people in the city knew about. They were escorted to a private table in the back of the room where Scott held her chair for her. The menu was in Chinese.

"A friend owns this place. If you don't mind, I'll order for us. Is there anything in particular you don't like?" Scott asked.

"No."

The waiter spoke with an accent. Jennifer smiled. It was obvious Scott knew him well. The two men conferred for several minutes comparing dishes. The man left with a smile and a promise to bring hot tea.

Jennifer relaxed. She was going to enjoy tonight.

The courses came and kept coming. A ceremonial teapot and small bowls of soup came first. The waiter placed a second larger bowl between them. "The soup is a type of sweet-and-sour soup, it has shrimp in it," Scott said. "The other dish is a house specialty. They are wontons cooked in a very spicy chicken broth. I'll warn you, they are very hot."

Jennifer carefully lifted one of the wontons from the dish. "These are delicious," she said after sampling the dish.

"I like them," Scott agreed.

The soup was followed by an assortment of fried rice dishes, a large platter of stir-fried vegetables, and then a shrimp and cashew dish that made Jennifer reach frequently for her water glass.

"I'm sorry. I should have ordered something less spicy."

"Are you kidding? This is wonderful. Jerry didn't like hot and spicy, and I love it."

Scott smiled and offered her one of the fresh-baked rolls to take away some of the effect.

She was going to make a wonderful wife, Scott thought, not for the first time. They had so much in common. Music, fishing, food. They both came from close families. Scott loved to listen to her laugh. She was relaxed tonight, and he was seeing Jennifer as she had been in the pictures before the death of Jerry and Colleen. Alive, happy. He could only hope she was drifting toward the same conclusion.

They left the restaurant almost two hours later. Scott held his jacket over her head as they ran to the car. It was barely raining, but it was an excuse to be near her. "I don't want to take you home," he admitted as he started the car.

Jennifer was grinning. "Let's go find somewhere to get a cup of coffee," she offered.

"Done."

He took them downtown to a five-star hotel that served gourmet coffee. At her suggestion they took the coffee into the atrium where a woman with a great voice played jazz standards at the piano. They settled into two comfortable chairs and shared a large chocolate chip cookie Scott had bought.

She was falling in love with him. Jennifer was laughing when the realization struck; Scott had retold a funny story he'd heard in Denver, and she had started to laugh. In that instant she knew she was falling in love with him. It was a sobering realization.

"Something wrong?"

She shook her head, absorbing the impact in her heart, and then she smiled, brilliantly. "Everything is fine."

It was almost midnight when they finally turned into her drive. Scott came around the car to open her door for her. He paused on the porch. "Jennifer."

She turned to look up at him, and he smiled. "Can I kiss you?"

It was a softly spoken query and it made her heart flutter. Jennifer wanted to blush, smile, put her arms around him. She simply nodded. Scott's hands very gently held her head and he lowered his head. The kiss held such tenderness that Jennifer nearly cried. She was smiling when he stepped back. Scott looked pleased. "You'd best get inside," he said huskily.

"Hi, Jerry." Jennifer sat down on the ground beside the headstone, her jeans and sweatshirt adequate protection for the cool, sunny afternoon. She had not been back to the grave site for over three months. She smiled sadly as she brushed the leaves from the smooth stone base. "I've got news I know you will be glad to hear."

She hugged her knees. She had woken up sad. "Scott's a good man. He makes me laugh. I miss him when he's not around. And it makes me incredibly sad, Jerry." She plucked at the dying grass. "We were suppose to have a lifetime together, you and I. I don't want to start over. How can love and sadness be so tightly intertwined?"

She glanced over at the second headstone, the reason she very rarely visited here. "Are you having a good time with your daddy, Colleen?" She asked, smiling, crying at the same time.

Chapter Ten

Jennifer watched the group of ten youths as they paired off and played pool, mentally putting names and faces together. Scott had encouraged her to join him for the pizza and pool, one of the events he was involved in organizing as a youth group sponsor. The kids ranged in age from twelve to seventeen, and as a whole were a close-knit, fun group. "The boy in the blue shirt at the far table playing by himself—what's his name?" Jennifer asked Scott's friend Trish as she surveyed the room from the vantage point of the long table and chairs, the remains of six large pizzas still around them.

"Kevin Philips. Fifteen."

"He's hurting," Jennifer commented, having formed the conclusion during the course of the evening. He had come across as angry and belligerent, and both Brad and Scott had spoken with him more than once. Jennifer looked below the surface, knowing there was a reason for the unreasonable behavior.

Trish nodded. "Adopted two years ago by Jim and Rita Philips. He'd been in foster care since he was seven, no place more than a year, had rough years before that in an abusive home."

"And now that he is in a safe and loving environment, he's letting himself feel the pain for the first time and he's angry," Jennifer concluded. "Giving Jim and Rita an extremely rough time in the process, I imagine."

"Got it in one," Trish replied.

"It must be like trying to hug a porcupine," Jennifer said thoughtfully.

Trish smiled, "Sad, isn't it?"

"Yeah," Jennifer agreed, making a decision. *God, I've got the faith to try. Do you have a way I can reach him?* She picked up her glass. "Can you hold the fort here? I think I'll see if there's a way around the needles."

"Beat him at pool. He disdains amateurs, but he'll respect a professional."

Jennifer looked surprised at the comment.

"You're the one who came in carrying a case with your own stick," Trish replied. "Have you played Scott yet?"

"No," Jennifer replied with a smile. She had been watching Scott play, and he was good, but he wasn't aggressive enough to deliberately take shots away from his opponent. She did it as naturally as breathing. She hadn't played tonight, but she had a feeling Scott would probably wander over to see what she could do.

"Be gentle with him," Trish said with a smile.

"Who? Scott or Kevin?"

"Kevin. Scott can take care of himself," Trish replied with a laugh.

It turned out to be as aggressive a game as Jennifer had imagined. Kevin had consented unwillingly to actually play a game with her. When she'd drilled her first shot and placed the seven into a pocket off the bank and left the cue ball six inches away from a certain second shot, she'd got a look of surprise from him, but he'd said nothing, simply turned his full attention to the game. Jennifer didn't mind. She hadn't come over to talk. Respect was a good common ground to forge, and the pool table was as good a place as any to forge it. She beat him the first game and ignored the fact the others were rotating around to play each other.

"Twenty bucks on the next game?" she asked quietly, pitching the triangle toward him.

"Ten to four balls, ten for the game," Kevin replied. "You've been playing a few years longer than I have."

Jennifer smiled. "Agreed." He was conceding a win would be difficult, but if he got the cue ball early it would be possible to hit a run of four balls. She liked the way he thought.

The game had his full concentration, and Jennifer had to admire the way he could tap a side rail shot. He got the break he had hoped for—her break had left the table open, and he took advantage to run the table. She saw the smile as he sank his fourth shot, saw the sense of accomplishment take away some of the anger and knew most of its joy came from the fact he had an opponent that wasn't willing to make a win easy for him. He missed a tough fifth shot. Jennifer peeled off a ten from the money in her pocket and handed it to him as she circled the table to look at what kind of shot, if any, she still had left to take.

Scott, walking toward them with a frown, disturbed her concentration but only for a moment. She focused on her shots, saw the angles and the force and began placing balls in the pockets with deliberation. She wasn't worried about making Kevin look bad, the better she played, the more that ten dollars was going to mean to him.

"Jen, can I talk to you for a moment?" Scott asked.

Jennifer called the hole for the eight ball and sank it before she looked up. Ouch. Scott was not happy.

"Kevin, buy us a plate of nachos and a couple colas. I'll be back in a minute," she told the teenager, who actually gave her a smile. She walked with Scott toward the side door.

"He's already got a gambling problem, Jen. The last thing we need is for a church youth group function to be fostering the problem."

"He earned the cash by his effort. Don't knock that sense of accomplishment."

"It's not good. Please, don't do it again."

Jennifer sighed. "Scott, he's going toe-to-toe with everyone around him, looking for who and what to respect. That cash is a trophy, not a gamble for thrill. He's met someone better than him at the pool table and he knows it, and he earned that ten bucks with his effort. It mattered to him. He may not show it, but it mattered to him."

Scott conceded she was right. "I'm glad to see the fact you got beneath his edge, I'll grant you that. But please, go cautious, Jen."

"Relax. An angry fifteen-year-old can still be managed. As long as you don't suggest that's what you're doing."

Jennifer went to join Kevin and the plate of super supreme nachos he'd bought and had to smile at the interest coming from the other kids. She knew the game they'd played had been observed and commented on, and the food would certainly garner at least the guys attention. She slid into the booth across from Kevin and picked up the soda. "Who taught you to play pool?" she asked the boy.

* * *

Scott slid out a chair at the end of the table where Trish and Brad were sitting so he could see the entire group of kids and keep an eye on Jennifer and Kevin sitting together in one of the booths.

"She wiped the table with him. Did you see that five, seven split shot she took and made?" Brad asked him, his respect apparent.

Scott smiled. "When she mentioned she played, she forgot to tell me she played seriously." He could not believe some of the shots she had attempted and made. He wouldn't even think to attempt them. He would ask her for a game later, just for the pleasure of watching her play.

"I like her, Scott," Trish said, watching her talk with Kevin.

"So do I," Scott replied. He was proud of her, proud of the way she had mingled with his friends and the group of kids. He might not agree with her actions, but he had to respect the fact she was willing to tackle the toughest kid in the group. He hoped she succeeded. It was important that someone reach Kevin and help him heal.

"Jennifer's place. Can I help you?"

Interesting. Who was this? Scott found the young girl's voice made him smile. "Hi, it's Scott Williams. Who is this?"

"Tiffany."

Sixth grade. Twelve years old. Thought Steve Sanders was the cutest boy on the planet. Was trying to make the track team this year. "Hi, Tiffany. Is your aunt Jennifer around?"

"She's out back with Dad working on the yard. I can get her for you," the girl offered.

"That's okay. You might be able to answer my question. She said she was looking for one of the Precious Moments figurines. It's a set of train cars with zoo animals. My sister found a couple of the pieces, and I don't remember if she said she was missing the giraffe or the lion."

"Hold on and I'll go look. I'd have to go look, anyway. Aunt Jennifer doesn't go into that room anymore."

Out of the mouth of babes. Jen still had the nursery. Scott felt sick.

The girl was back in a few moments. "It's the giraffe."

Scott rubbed the tension is his forehead and tried to keep his voice light. "Thanks."

"Sure. Can I ask you something?"

He smiled. "Of course."

"Are you really getting a dog? 'Cause I'd love to visit, and Aunt Jen talks about you all the time, and I thought it might be okay to ask."

Scott grinned. "I get Quigley in a couple days. Tell your aunt Jen you've got to come. I would love to have you over. I'll need someone to baby-sit him when I have to be out of town, and Jen will need your help."

"Cool. I knew I was going to like you."

"Tell Jennifer I'll call her this evening," Scott said, pleased to have finally talked to the girl Jennifer bragged about with such love.

He hung up the phone, and Heather reached over to grip his arm. "What's wrong?" She was sorting the baby clothes she had found at garage sales that morning, the figurines she had also found sitting on the counter beside the clothes.

"Twig, she's still got the nursery. And according to her niece, Tiffany, she won't even walk into the room anymore. Tiffany said it in such a matter-of-fact tone of voice, like it's been this way for some time."

"You need to talk to her brother."

"Yeah. I do." Scott wearily rubbed his eyes. It had been a

bad week at work, and it wasn't getting better on a personal level, either. The anger between him and God still sat there, tempered with time, but there and needing to be dealt with.

"Would you like to stay for dinner? I really appreciate you watching Greg and Amy for me."

Scott grinned. "You know I always have as much fun as your kids. Greg's turning into a good basketball player. I'll take a rain check on dinner, though, I've got mail to deal with and a youth group lesson to prepare. Frank gets back in town tomorrow?"

"His flight comes in around six, so it will be just me and the kids at church tomorrow morning."

"Plan for us to go out for lunch. I promised Amy pizza."

"Thanks."

Scott kissed his sister's cheek. "You're welcome. Now get off your feet, Twig, you're seriously pregnant."

She laughed and pushed him toward the door.

Quigley found his new home fascinating. Jennifer, sitting on the floor in the doorway of Scott's kitchen, watched the puppy circle the furniture in the dining room, suddenly turn and come full-speed back toward her when he got frightened by a dust ball. Jennifer caught him with a laugh. "What's the matter, little guy?" He was pure black, furry, his face too big for the rest of his body. He licked her face.

"I think he likes you." Scott had leaned over the counter to peer down at the two of them. He was grinning.

"I want to take him home," Jennifer replied, snuggling with the puppy.

"Sorry. You'll just have to visit often to see him," Scott replied. He came around and offered a helping hand to pull her to her feet. "Lunch is ready."

"I have to put him down?" Jennifer asked with regret.

"If you don't, he will eat your lunch," Scott replied. "I know, he's done it to me a few times." Scott took the puppy, and Quigley immediately made himself comfortable, resting his head on Scott's shoulder.

"No, I'd say you don't carry him around very much."

"He likes to go fishing," Scott replied.

Jennifer laughed and followed Scott to the patio for lunch. It was an Indian summer day, comfortably warm, not even a jacket necessary. Scott had fixed brats out on the grill. He set Quigley down and clipped on the hundred-foot leash so Quigley could go exploring without getting lost.

"Can you tolerate the onions?" Scott asked as he loaded his brat with condiments.

"What?"

"If we are going to be kissing, do you want onions on my breath or not?"

She slid her arm around his waist as she reached around him for the mustard. "Taking a lot for granted, aren't you?"

He turned and kissed her. Both his hands were full, but he did an adequate job. "Nope."

"Go light on the onions," she requested, smiling.

The sadness was gone. She was in love with him, and she didn't mind if he suspected as much. For now, she just liked being with him. They needed some time together as friends.

Scott handed her a soda and a napkin, and Jennifer settled back in the patio chair to watch Quigley and laugh with Scott at his antics.

"I promised Tiffany she could come meet Quigley, so let me know what day might be good and you can invite Peter and Rachel and the kids over and we'll have a cookout."

"Scott."

She was going to protest that it wasn't good to bring family into the relationship this early but Scott didn't let her finish. Her family was likely going to be his most powerful ally. "If you won't ask them, I will." There was a twinkle in his eyes as he said it, but also the seriousness of his intentions.

"I'll talk to Rachel," Jennifer finally agreed.

They went walking on the beach later that afternoon. Scott let Quigley run without a leash. The puppy scampered around, flirting with the water's edge, pausing occasionally to dig furiously in the sand. "You're going to have to give him a bath when we get back to the house," Jennifer commented.

"He kind of likes the blow-dryer—hates the noise, but likes to put his face in the warm air," Scott replied.

Scott's arm was around Jennifer's back, her arm was around his waist. He liked afternoons like this. If he got his way, there would be many more of them. He loved her. He no longer questioned that. It was only a matter of time now before he made that declaration. He figured the more afternoons they had together like this, the easier it would be for Jennifer to answer him.

"You want to come to Greg's birthday party Saturday? He's going to be nine. You could meet my folks. You've met everyone else in the family," he said.

He watched her bite her bottom lip. "Your parents?"

"They are going to love you," he said with a smile. "We'll bring Quigley along, too, for a puppy reunion. What do you say, Jen?"

Jennifer tilted her head to look up at him. She hesitated. "Sure. Why not?"

He leaned down and kissed her, slowly, taking his time. He could feel her smiling, and he was ready to haul her back to the patio chair where he could do it properly, when Quigley decided he needed to shower them with sand. "Quig, you've got to learn better timing," Scott protested. Jennifer just laughed.

* * *

She shouldn't have come.

Jennifer watched Scott in the backyard of Heather and Frank's home playing with six kids and four puppies and felt the joy of the last month disappear.

She shouldn't have come. There was no denying reality any longer. In a month of loving him, she had conveniently been ignoring one very obvious fact. Scott was going to want to have kids. Heather stopped beside her at the dining room table, smiled with her at the antics outside. "The kids are having a great time with the puppies." Greg had invited four of his school friends over for the party.

"Yes. They are all having a great time," Jennifer agreed. She was trying her best to not think about how pregnant Heather was. She liked Scott's sister a lot. Heather was a wealth of stories about Scott, and Jennifer wasn't above looking for information. Heather's due date was only two weeks away now, and as much as Jennifer liked her, she was doing her best not to think about the baby. Jennifer felt Heather look over at her and forced herself to shift back to a carefree appearance. "Can I help with the cake?"

"Mom is finding the candles. Then it's just a matter of calling the kids inside," Heather replied. They watched the antics in the backyard for a few more moments, then Heather slid open the patio door and stepped outside to call everyone in for cake.

Scott's mom joined Jennifer and smiled at the scene in the backyard. "I don't know who is enjoying themselves more, Scott or the kids. Amy and Greg are both having a great time."

Jennifer turned to smile at Margaret. Scott's mom had made her feel welcome from the moment she had walked in the door, and Jennifer was relieved. Margaret had looked at the way Scott had his arm around her, looked at the expression on Scott's face, and when she'd turned to look at Jennifer the deck had already been stacked in her favor. "Scott does seem to like kids," Jennifer said after a moment, dreading the second confirmation and knowing she had to hear it.

"That he does. He'll make a good father."

Jennifer nodded but didn't reply.

Scott came inside with the children, carrying his niece, Amy, in one arm and Quigley in the other, laughing over something Amy had told him. Jennifer smiled when Scott reached her, took the offered Quigley. Amy looked so right in his arms. The little girl had her arms around Scott's neck and was clearly very pleased to be where she was. Amy had been at the door to meet them, been hoisted up by her uncle Scott for a smooch and had given Jennifer a wide grin and asked Scott if this was his girlfriend, like Jeff was her boyfriend. Scott had frowned and had wanted to know when he had been bumped as her boyfriend, and Amy had just giggled and explained that Scott didn't have a hamster and Jeff did.

Quigley chose that moment to stick his nose in her face, and Jennifer laughed and shifted him around so he could rest like a football in her arms. She loved this puppy. Scott hoisted Amy into one of the chairs and came back to join Jennifer. He stepped out of the way by standing behind her. He draped his arms around her waist, rested his chin against her shoulder. "How do you like my parents?" he whispered in her ear.

"I like them both," she whispered back. His dad had given her a hug and told her to make sure Scott behaved himself, that he was dangerous at birthday parties.

The dining room table was set with party decorations,

streamers, balloons, party napkins and cups. After "Happy Birthday" was sung, the candles blown out, the cake was cut and passed around. Since Jennifer was still holding Quigley, Scott shared his piece with her. Jennifer giggled when he got icing on her chin. "Hold still," Scott warned as he lowered his head. She knew he had done it deliberately so he would have an excuse to kiss her.

"Don't you dare," she whispered fiercely. She didn't mind his family seeing them holding hands. Kissing was another matter. Scott grinned and rubbed the icing off with his finger instead.

"Scott, would you and Jennifer like some ice cream to go with that cake?" His mom's question had a touch of laughter in it. Jennifer blushed.

"Thanks, Mom, but I think we're okay with just the cake," Scott replied, not minding the question and not looking away from Jennifer. He hadn't seen this shade of pink before. It was quite endearing.

It was late. After midnight. Jennifer tossed another wadded tissue toward the bathroom trash can. She was sitting in the tub, crying her eyes out, and she was beginning to get mad.

Scott was going to want to have children.

What was she going to do?

She had tried to call Beth, but her friend wasn't home, and she didn't want to call Rachel. Not yet. Rachel would talk to Peter, and Peter would want to put his arms around her and fix it, and when he couldn't it would make him more sad, and Jennifer knew her brother had already carried more pain than any man should ever be expected to carry. The memory of his face as a pallbearer for Colleen was the last pain she ever wanted to cause him. The whole problem was the fact this couldn't be fixed.

It was a horrible dilemma. She was in love with him. But even the idea of having children petrified her. Jennifer couldn't think about children without thinking about the hospital, the doctors, the fear. The funeral. Colleen had struggled so hard to live. Jennifer didn't have the strength to risk losing another child.

How could she think about marrying Scott, when she knew she was going to deny him the fulfillment of his dream? She couldn't risk having another child. Not even for Scott. She was petrified of the idea. The tears came harder, and Jennifer gave up trying to stop them. She felt as if her heart was breaking. She loved him. And she was going to have to give him up.

Jennifer finally got hold of her friend Beth early the next morning. If anyone was going to be able to help her sort through what she had to do, it was Beth. Jennifer had reached the horrible conclusion that her only option was to say goodbye to Scott and not see him anymore. "Beth, could I fly out and see you and Les for a few days?" Jennifer asked when her friend answered the phone. Twenty minutes later, she stepped into a cab for a ride to the airport.

Scott paced the corridor of the airport terminal, waiting for Jennifer's flight to get in. To say he'd been surprised when she called from South Dakota was to understate his reaction. He had been trying to reach her for two days when she had called. Something was wrong. Jennifer hadn't said anything on the phone, only that she was visiting a friend, but Scott didn't need to be told that something had sent her running. Jennifer was not the type to simply up and leave without a reason.

Her flight finally landed, twenty minutes late. Scott was standing at the gate as the passengers entered the terminal. He saw her immediately. She looked exhausted, her eyes dark, her expression weary and sad.

"Hi, Jen." He took her carry-on bag and wondered if she would accept a hug. She removed the uncertainty by stepping forward to hug him. "Thanks for coming, Scott."

Okay. Whatever was wrong, it was at least going to be fixable. Scott held her tight, grateful to have her back. She'd scared him leaving like that and he took a deep breath and let it out slowly. "Have you eaten yet?"

"Yes. The food on the plane was not too bad."

"Let's get your luggage then, and I'll take you home." He kept an arm around her as they walked down the terminal to the baggage claims area. "How's Beth?"

"Beth is fine. I'm glad I went. The phone simply doesn't do a close friendship justice." Jennifer pointed out her one bag. Scott got her luggage and led her out to the car.

"Jen, why did you go?" Scott asked after several minutes of silence in the car. He had debated whether he wanted to ask the question or not, he was afraid of the answer, but he found the need to know was stronger than the fear.

"I needed to talk about Colleen," Jennifer finally replied. She turned and looked at him. "Beth knows the terrain. She lost a son in a drunk driving accident."

"How did it go?"

"Okay." Jennifer gave a half smile. "I cried a lot. Be glad you were not there."

Scott reached over and grasped her hand. "Don't. Don't hide the pain, Jen. It matters that you let me be part of this recovery."

She squeezed his hand. "I'm sorry. I know you want to help." Jennifer bit her lip. "I'm scared of having children again, Scott. Really, really scared."

His eyes closed briefly. No. Not this. Anything but this. He had been afraid she felt that way about children, but had hoped time had made her feelings less intense. Scott urged her over to sit beside him so he could put his arm around her. "It must be a very frightening idea to consider, after what happened with Colleen." His voice was husky, and he found it hard to speak. He could tell how much pain Jen was in, and he was sharing it. They had to be able to have children together. They had to.

"I keep remembering the hospital delivery room and the neonatal intensive care and the way she didn't breathe. The image is frozen in my mind."

Scott felt Jennifer take a deep breath. "I'm getting past the fear. I've got to. That's one of the reasons I went to see Beth."

Scott heard the determination in her voice and was so grateful she was working to heal. "What can I do to help?" he asked huskily, willing to do anything he could.

Jennifer eased her hand more firmly into Scott's. She loved him. She could do this. She could face having children again. Beth had helped make that choice clear. If she wanted a life with Scott, she was going to face her fears and deal with them. The bottom-line conclusion was simple. She loved Scott too much to let him go. A week with a friend who knew she could do it had helped make that decision possible. "Just be there, Scott. I'm going to beat this fear," she replied.

"Do you need a jacket?" he asked. Jennifer had on a sweatshirt, but the breeze off the lake was cool tonight.

"No, I'm fine," Jennifer replied. She had been home a

week since she'd gone to see Beth, and her courage to at least consider children was still intact. She had begun to think about the possibility more, had actually got up the nerve to go into the room that had been set up as Colleen's nursery and sit for a while. Scott had invited her to his place for dinner and a walk on the beach tonight. She thought it was a good sign that he had let her drive over instead of coming to pick her up. The laughter of the last month had disappeared and been replaced with something more serious, more intense. The fun of a friendship was still there, but there were larger issues in front of them now, and they both knew it.

"Did you get much done on the book today?" Scott asked quietly as they began their walk along the beach, Quigley racing out ahead of them.

"I wrote about six pages. A moderately good day, I guess. I normally want to write about ten. How was work?"

Scott smiled. "Every problem in the entire company seemed to come across my desk today," he replied. "I was glad I had tonight to look forward to."

"Dinner was very good." He had made a thick beef stew.

He hugged her. "You're willing to taste my experiments. That must be one of the signs of a good friend."

"If you make something really bad, I probably will have to tell you," Jennifer replied with a smile. She bent down and found a smooth rock, sent it skipping over the water. "You must love having the water so close."

"I do. It is a very peaceful walk." Quigley chose that moment to coming running back to stop beside them, tail wagging, proceeding to shake all the sand off his coat. "Quigley, behave yourself," Scott said sternly, having to hide his grin. The puppy just nudged his leg. "If you find a stick, I'll throw it," Scott told the dog. Quigley took off down the beach again.

They had not talked directly about children since the car ride back from the airport. Jennifer did not want to broach the subject, and Scott fully intended to give her all the time she needed.

They walked back to the house forty minutes later, holding hands.

Jennifer found Quigley's brush and began to brush the sand out of his hair while Scott went to check for any messages.

"Jennifer." She looked up to see Scott in the patio doorway. "Heather has been admitted, in labor. Mom's message said they are planning to do the C-section at 7:00 p.m. That's just about now."

Jennifer felt part of her stomach drop. She wasn't ready for this kind of test yet. Not yet. She let Quigley climb from her lap and got up and dusted off her jeans. "Since my car is here, let's both drive to the hospital," she said, getting a firm grip on her courage.

Scott came to join her, tilting up her chin so he could see her eyes. "Are you sure?" he asked, worried.

Jennifer forced a smile. "I'm sure. Let me get my purse, and we can be on our way."

Scott hesitated, then nodded. "All right. I'll lock up the house."

Jennifer followed him to the hospital. If it had been the same hospital as where she had had Colleen, Jennifer would never have turned into the parking lot. As it was, she pulled in and parked beside Scott and found her hands were damp with sweat.

They walked across the parking lot to the main entrance of the hospital, followed the signs to the elevators that would take them to the fourth floor and maternity. Jennifer suddenly balked when the elevators opened and Scott moved to step inside. "I can't do this." She shook her head wildly, feeling the panic. She had spent too much time in her past on a maternity ward floor, in the intensive care. She couldn't go up there. The hospital smell was already making her stomach churn. She couldn't go up there and wait for a baby to be born. What if she were bad luck and the baby died?

Scott grabbed her in a bear hug, stopping a panicked flight. "Easy. Jen, it's okay. We're not going up there," he said firmly. She was shaking uncontrollably. "Come on." He walked her toward the hospital doors, waving aside a concerned front desk attendant and got her outside. He found them a private alcove where he could lean against a pillar and hold her.

She started to calm down. "Scott, I'm so sorry. I thought I could do this." She was crying, and he found a handkerchief and carefully wiped her eyes.

"It's okay, Jen. I saw when the panic hit. You did okay for several minutes. I bet that is better than you've done before," he said quietly.

"It is. But still. It's just a hospital."

"Don't beat yourself up. It's not going to help," Scott said softly. He was suddenly getting a firsthand taste of what he was battling, and the assumptions that he'd made were all proving woefully inadequate. "Come on, Jen. Let me take you home."

"No. You need to go be with your family. I live less than a mile from here. I can drive home."

"No way."

She smiled at his firm tone. "Yes. I'll be fine. Your family needs you upstairs."

He halfway conceded. "I'll follow you home and make sure you get there safely, then come back," he replied.

She nodded her agreement, because there was going to be no way to dissuade him and walked with him to her car. He followed immediately behind her as she drove to her house. Scott got out and came up to the front door with her.

"Will you call me when you have news?" Jennifer asked him. She hated the fact she wasn't going to be there with him.

"I'll call you." Scott gently kissed her. "Please, don't think about kids tonight. Don't beat yourself up. Promise me?"

There were tears in her eyes as she nodded. "I promise," she whispered.

The phone rang at 9:00 p.m. Jennifer had gone to bed but was awake, snuggled under the covers, thinking. Her eyes were dry. She had checked the tears by force of will. She didn't know how to process what had happened, and the intense sadness was overwhelming. She'd had no idea that the fear had burned so deep inside, until she'd tried to walk past it.

"Heather had a baby girl. Mary Elizabeth. Seven pounds. Both of them are doing fine."

Jennifer squeezed her eyes shut and let out a deep sigh of relief. "Thank you, Scott. That's the best news you could have told me."

"How are you doing, Jen?" She could hear the controlled pain in his voice, the fact he wasn't coping with what had happened any better than she was.

"I'll be okay, Scott." She struggled to put some confidence in the words that she didn't feel.

"Can I come by?" She heard the plea and closed her eyes. She had heard that plea before on the beach the first morning, and she had pushed him away then, and she was going to be forced to do it again and it was killing her. She couldn't talk right now, not until she dealt with the churn inside and could talk from some sort of level perspective.

"I've already turned in for the night. Could we get together tomorrow?"

His silence was so pain filled. Why did things have to be like this? Why did she have to hurt him like this? It was going to get worse, not better, and it was killing her. "I'll call you. We can go out for dinner and a movie," Scott offered.

"I'll look forward to it, Scott."

She hung up the phone after they said goodbye. Rubbed her eyes. It was there, staring them both in the face. The uncertainty of whether the relationship was going to survive. Prayer. She needed to pray.

Lord, I panicked. Deep inside, I panicked. And I couldn't control it. And I wanted out. And if I'd had to abandon Scott to get away I would have done it. What am I suppose to do now? It's there. It's not moving. I felt death tonight, felt the same icy chill of death I felt as I sat beside Colleen's incubator and realized she had not taken another breath. I can't fight death. I don't have that kind of courage. If it's going to stay there, sitting inside, cold and unyielding, I've got no choice but to tell Scott goodbye.

Scott walked the beach with Quigley late that night. If a few tears slipped that no one could see, they went unnoticed. Jennifer was hurting so badly. And he so badly wanted them to be able to have children.

Chapter Eleven

❧

It was late when Scott arrived at Jennifer's to pick her up for dinner. He'd been forced to call her from work and move the time, when a late crisis in the day had necessitated another meeting. Andrew had been there at the meeting, and Scott knew his presence had saved him. He'd just about blown his temper at a line supervisor, and Andrew had stepped in and prevented it from happening. The guy had been wrong, but it had only been a mistake, not malicious, and blowing his temper would have been a lousy way to present himself.

He needed a break from this. He needed the pain to go away.

Lord, don't let the anger blow toward Jennifer. It's the situation that's triggering the anger, the fear inside, but she'll see it as her fault. I'm frustrated that there is so much left to do for Jennifer to heal. So much more time needed, so much fear inside me that we won't have children. What if it doesn't work out? What if Jennifer can't heal? What do we do then?

Scott parked the car and turned off the ignition and deliberately rested his hands across the steering wheel.

Lord, it's not going inside the house with me, this emotion. We both need a break. So take it, Lord, and help me give her what we both need, faith that You'll take care of this. Please.

Jen opened the front door when he knocked, and Scott was grateful to see the calmness in her brown eyes. She was in better shape than he had expected. He stepped inside and hugged her, and she hugged him back.

"I went ahead and fixed us dinner since I didn't know what time you might get free. I really would prefer to stay in tonight," she said as she took his coat.

"You can cook?" he teased, and she swatted his arm. "Well I didn't know. Not everyone can." He tugged her back into his arms as an apology. "What did you fix?"

"Pizza. And yes, I made it from the crust up. It's good."

"It smells delicious." He meant it. He could smell the yeast in the dough rising as the crust cooked, the cheese melting.

She leaned back in his arms. "Let's not talk about it tonight, okay? Not kids, not the panic, not Colleen. Not any of it."

His eyes closed when she made the request, and he rested his forehead against her hair. The sigh came from deep inside. Thank you, Lord. They needed time more than they needed words. "You have a deal." He smiled, not moving his head from where it rested against her hair. "But only if I get control of the TV remote." He'd known it would get a smile, but he hadn't counted on the gentle elbow in his ribs.

"Hey."

"At least Jerry would flip me for it."

He picked her up.

"A quarter, Scott, not literally." She was laughing, and it was the first time he'd heard the sound in a long time. It was a beautiful sound. Scott lowered her feet back to the floor and gently kissed her.

"Check the pizza and let's go surf the channels for something funny to watch."

They said nothing profound the whole evening, just sat on the floor in front of the couch and ate great pizza and laughed at old episodes of "Coach," and "Murphy Brown," and watched Doris Day and Cary Grant fall in love, and occasionally Scott would lean over and kiss Jennifer just for the pleasure of the contact.

Scott was traveling to San Francisco for a conference. The plane was somewhere over the Rockies and the view out the window was breathtaking, but he wasn't enjoying it. A folder was open in his lap and yet to be read; his mind wasn't on work, even though he was presenting a session.

The stress he had seen in her eyes was killing him. Jennifer was in so much pain. If only he could truthfully tell her he didn't want children. All this pain would go away. But he couldn't tell her that. He really wanted a family.

He needed to call her, just to hear her voice. Make sure she hadn't run. She was feeling so guilty, feeling like the fear was her fault. But it wasn't. Scott could see in her pain how badly the trauma of Colleen's death had affected her. The fear was a natural protective measure against the pain, and it was the pain that was the enemy.

He thought about three dates swiftly approaching, Thanksgiving, the anniversary of Colleen's death—he winced at that one—and Christmas. And he knew all of them were going to be hard on Jennifer. He couldn't keep hurting her. He had to let the pain go and give her the time she needed to heal. He had to keep the faith that she would be able to heal.

He was gone four days, and when he returned, it was to find Jennifer's message on his machine saying she was going to need to cancel their dinner date for the next night, that her editor needed her to turn around some revisions to the last Thomas Bradford book overnight. He listened to the message and rubbed his hand over his face and wished he could call her and be the lighthearted friend she so badly needed. Whenever he called her now he seemed to only add to the pain she felt; he was the reminder now of her fear and it haunted him.

Scott reluctantly didn't call her. They needed to be married. He needed to be able to hold her and not let her go, and if they couldn't talk, at least they could share the silence.

The house was empty and lonely. Knowing the pile of work at the office after four days of being gone was going to be steep, Scott decided he might as well spend two hours at the office getting started on the work he had to do. Work didn't take his mind off the problems, but it at least forced him to keep moving.

She couldn't put off talking to Scott about children any longer.

Jennifer sat beside him at the Thanksgiving table, watched him with his family and knew she couldn't put off talking to him any longer. She loved him, and he wanted a family, and she knew the reality. He thought time was helping. It was going to kill her to admit the reality to him. She hid her troubled thoughts as best she could. Scott was relaxed, and she didn't want to rob him of that today.

The guys went out back to play some basketball after dinner, and Jennifer smiled as she watched them. Heather joined her, carrying a now-awake Mary Elizabeth. She was just finishing a bottle.

"How's she doing?" Jennifer asked, envious.

"Quite well. She is a very even-tempered baby. She only gets me up twice during the night," Heather replied with a smile, turning down the blanket so Jennifer could see her little hands.

"Could I hold her?" Jennifer asked, surprising herself.

"Sure," Heather replied. She slid the bottle to one side and handed Jennifer the second cloth diaper she was carrying. "She needs to burp."

Very carefully, Jennifer took the infant. The infant was waving her arms, trying to smile, with bright blue eyes and full cheeks, there was nothing frail or premature about her. She weighed double what Colleen had ever weighed. Jennifer eased the infant onto her shoulder and gently patted her back.

Jennifer grinned when the baby took a fistful of her hair and started to tug. "You find this very tempting, don't you, honey?" She gently loosened the baby's grip. It felt so wonderful to be holding a baby again. Jennifer blinked away tears that threatened to fall. She wasn't going to cry. She wasn't.

She tried to think about what it would be like to be pregnant again, have her own baby, and the joy she felt turned to almost panic. Mary Elizabeth suddenly looked like Colleen. Jennifer blinked hard and forced herself to take a deep breath. "Thank you, Heather." Jennifer handed Mary Elizabeth back carefully, grateful for the chance to hold her, her smile sad, knowing what she had just learned was going to change things for the worst.

"Jennifer, I'm sorry."

Heather did understand the tears that threatened to fall, and Jennifer gave her a tremulous smile. "You have a beautiful baby, Heather," she said, fighting for her composure.

The game outside began to break up. Jennifer forced the sadness away.

Scott came in with a smile, tugged Jennifer down beside him on the couch in the living room to watch the football game with him, kept her tucked firmly under his arm for the rest of the day. Jennifer loved him for it, for the comfort his presence brought.

They left his parents' house early in the evening. Scott took Jennifer home, and at her request came in for coffee. He leaned down to kiss her as they entered the house, and she tipped her head back and let the kiss deepen, feeling desperate. She loved him so much. She would give anything not to have to say what she had to say.

She was going to be breaking his heart and be breaking hers, and she dreaded what the next year was going to be like without him, and she wanted to cry and plead with God to change this, but the pleading was done, and the crying was done, and this was the reality she was going to have to live with. Holding Mary Elizabeth had forced her to face the irrevocable truth. She was afraid to have children again. *Too* afraid to ever change.

He knew something was wrong. His face was serious, his hands gentle on her waist. "Would you fix the coffee? I need to find something," she asked. He hesitated, then nodded.

Jennifer looked through the video tapes she had collected over the years, bit her lip as she found the tapes tied together with a blue ribbon. God, I need some courage, she said silently, opening the ribbon. She found the first tape she wanted and slid it into the machine, picked up the remote.

Scott came in with the coffee, and Jennifer nodded toward the couch. "Old movie night?" he asked quietly. Jennifer curled up beside him.

"I thought you might like to meet Jerry and Colleen," she replied. She felt Scott's sudden look of surprise, but she didn't look over at him. She turned on the tape.

Scott didn't say a word; he did put his arm around her.

Nervous was not a good enough term to describe how Jennifer was feeling. "The sound is not very good on this first part. It was taken at his bachelor party."

"There's Jerry on the couch." Jennifer indicated as the camera panned across the living room packed with people. "The man on his left is his best man. This was taken about a week before our wedding. Finals had just gotten over the day before. It's a Friday night, most of his college buddies stayed around to help him celebrate. They did a great job setting Jerry up. He thought we were going out to dinner and came over to the dorm to pick me up. Instead, he walked into four of his buddies who escorted him to the party."

Scott, watching the man on the screen, laughing with his friends, felt real envy. The man was a gifted speaker. Watching him, after catcalls of "speech," get up and off-the-cuff do a five-minute talk on why he was forsaking bachelorhood for marriage, made Scott realize just how much Jerry had loved Jennifer.

Jerry returned puns with his friends as he unwrapped the gifts. Items wrapped in the best bachelor fashion: brown paper bags. Tape was the first gift. "To ensure I keep my mouth shut at all appropriate times." Glue; a waste can. "If I can't fix it, I can always throw it away." Antacids. "No comment. Jennifer is bound to see this movie one day." A plunger. Jerry had dissolved into laughter when he saw that one. "Cute, guys. Real cute." A spade. "For shoveling out the dirt Jennifer likes to brush under the rug."

The last package was actually wrapped in real blue and gold wrapping paper. Jerry opened it, obviously puzzled. He turned deep red. A pair of blue boxer shorts.

"My gift," Jennifer admitted to Scott, her own face feeling hot.

Scott squeezed her arm, having heard the admission.

The next part of the video was from the wedding reception. Watching Jennifer and her new husband, Jerry, greeting friends, sharing cake, opening gifts, made Scott grow more and more silent. He was becoming more and more aware of just how much Jennifer had lost.

Jennifer changed the tape. "This is at the hospital with Colleen." Scott realized suddenly that in the past few months with Jennifer she had never shown him Colleen's picture. He leaned forward as the tape showed the hospital nursery. "Peter was taking the pictures?" he asked quietly. Jennifer nodded.

Colleen was a pretty baby, small, fragile, but all the more beautiful because of it. She had such tiny hands. Watching Jennifer hold her daughter made Scott feel like crying. He could see the bond between them. No wonder Jennifer had not shown him this tape before. He looked over, saw that Jennifer was silently crying. He wrapped his arm around her shoulder.

The tape eventually ended.

"That's Colleen."

He reached over and gently kissed her wet cheek. "Thanks for sharing her, Jen," he whispered softly.

She nodded. She took a deep breath. "We need to talk." She looked at him, looked away. "I don't want to have any more children. I can't do it."

She felt him freeze. She went on before her courage failed her. "I've tried my best. I even managed to hold Mary Elizabeth today. But I can't do it. I can't have children again. I can't risk going through the loss of a child again."

"Jen, the odds of that happening again..."

She shook her head. "To live with that kind of fear is something I can't do."

He hugged her toward him, rested his chin on the top of her head. "I know you've been thinking about this for some time. Is this definite? Will more time help?"

"It's definite, Scott." She was crying. "I am so sorry."

He brushed back the tears. He was silent for some time. "I really want to have children with you, Jen."

"I can't take that risk again, Scott. I just can't," she whispered brokenly.

The hard part was, he did understand.

Chapter Twelve

❧

She wasn't going to answer the phone.

The machine picked up after four rings, and Scott left Jennifer another message for her to call him. She didn't want to talk to him. She was trying to put distance between them, and it was killing him to realize that was what she was doing.

What was he going to do?

Since that night three days ago, when she had said she couldn't risk having children again, his thoughts, his emotions, had swung in all directions. He wanted children. He wanted to have a family. She knew it, and in her own way she was trying to say goodbye.

Anger driving him to his feet, Scott left his office and paced through his house. Why did this have to happen? Why? It made no sense. God was supposed to be able to heal grief, give courage, but Jennifer had not healed. And his hope, his optimism which had been that time would heal the trauma and Jennifer would eventually accept the idea of having a child again, was up against a brick wall. Scott knew Jennifer's decision wasn't going to change. She couldn't risk losing a child again. It wasn't a matter of giving her another year, the trauma had irreversibly set her decision.

He honestly did understand. She couldn't risk losing a child again. But understanding did not lessen his own pain. He wanted children. He wanted a family. And he was now facing the loss of his own dream. No children. He was feeling the pain Jennifer must have felt when she lost Colleen. It felt like his heart was breaking.

Needing the space, Scott called for Quigley and headed for the beach.

Her decision had placed him at the point he was going to have to make a decision of his own.

He could begin to look for another lady to be his wife. If he wanted a family, that was his option. In his head he knew that, but the thought lingered only long enough for his heart to response. He loved Jennifer. There was no way he could walk away from her.

That left only the toughest road—to deal with his own grief of not having a family and reach the point where he could accept that cost. It made Scott painfully aware of what he would never have. An infant of his own to hold, rock to sleep, teach to walk. There would be no son or daughter racing to the door when he got home from work, eager to be picked up and hugged.

He could adjust to that reality. Eventually. He knew he could. If Jennifer gave him the chance. She might walk away from him for good rather than let him sacrifice his dream for a family. She had that kind of courage inside, and it scared Scott.

God, why did you do this? Why did Colleen die? Why

did you let Jennifer get so badly hurt? Why am I being asked to lose my dream of a family?

The emotions tore into his words, and he stormed the beach for over an hour until his legs were spent and the anger was spent and one decision was burned into stone. He was not walking away from her.

Okay, God. What are we going to do?

The prayer came from his gut as he stopped at the top of a rise and looked out over the water. He had had his back to the wall before, and God had gotten him out, there had to be some plan for this time.

He didn't know enough.

He had seen the episode at the hospital, had seen the panic suddenly hit her. He knew she was afraid. But what specifically was she afraid of? What triggered the terror? Was it being pregnant? Was it the age of the child? Was it the hospital experience? Was she afraid of a second marriage, as well, losing another husband? He needed answers, because one thing was clear inside.

He was *not* walking away.

"Jennifer, can I get you anything else? A cup of hot tea maybe?" Rachel asked as she stopped beside the recliner where Jennifer was watching the kids play outside in the snow.

"Thanks, Rachel, but I'm okay for now," Jennifer replied, grateful for her friend's concern. In the past three days a cold had settled deep into her chest. The stress of the severed relationship with Scott was taking its toll on her mood as well as her physical health.

Tiffany, Alexander and Tom were all having fun out in the snow. It was not much, only a light dusting, but it was enough to enjoy. Jennifer smiled sadly as she watched them play.

Her decision had been the only one she could make, but that didn't make the pain less. She had been ducking Scott's calls the past few days, afraid he might try to change her mind. Afraid to let him close. She had not told Peter and Rachel what had happened, but her friend seemed to know. Jennifer thought she had masked her grief about Colleen, but it was apparent Rachel at least suspected the truth.

"Christmas is three weeks away, and I've still got so much to do," Rachel said as she came back into the living room and took a seat beside Jennifer. "Christmas cookies and decorations and presents to buy." She smiled. "I love it. You are still planning to come for Christmas Eve, aren't you?"

"I wouldn't miss it," Jennifer said with a smile. "Can I bring anything?"

"Scott," Rachel replied, and Jennifer felt her smile stiffen. Three weeks from now Scott might not even be talking to her. "I'll ask him," she told Rachel.

It was so tough to love someone. She had to consider what was best for Scott, and she wasn't best for him anymore. She shivered. The thought of losing another child terrified her. She so desperately wanted him in her life, but not if it cost him his own dreams for a family. She would regret forever letting him give up his dreams.

"He's a good man, Jen," Rachel said, watching her.

"Yes, he is," Jennifer agreed, a catch in her voice. She paused to cough hard, feeling like her lungs were going to tear apart.

Jennifer smiled as her niece and nephews came bundling into the house, crowded around to ask if she had seen them make their snow angels. She loved these three kids. "Would a kiss make your cold better?" Tiffany asked as she pulled off her gloves.

"It might help," Jennifer offered, and Tiffany threw her

cold hands around Jennifer's neck and gave her a big kiss on the cheek. "I want you to get better."

There were tears in Jennifer's eyes as she hugged the girl. "Thank you, munchkin."

"Jennifer."

She paused at the front door and turned, surprised. Scott. He was here. For five days she had avoided answering the phone, had played his messages and forced herself to not reply. She had hoped if she could make him angry, he would feel the pain less. And still he had come. She watched him walk up the front drive and her eyes looked at him, hungrily, having missed him so badly. He looked as rough as she felt. He had not had a good five days. "Scott. Why are you here?" she asked quietly as he joined her.

He took the keys from her hand and unlocked her front door. "To talk to you. Not answering my calls is not going to make the problem go away," he replied firmly, pushing open the door. He waited for her to precede him. She could see the determination in his face. He wanted to talk.

Jennifer tried to shore up her resolve and walked into the house before him. Ignoring him, she went into the kitchen, took off her coat and found a glass. She had been to see the doctor, and his diagnosis of walking pneumonia had somehow seemed fitting. She felt terrible. Scott was in the kitchen doorway watching her, as she opened the prescription bottle she had picked up from the pharmacy and swallowed the pills. She tipped her glass toward him. "Would you like something to drink?"

"A stiff drink seems fitting, but I'll fix some coffee later," Scott replied. He was looking at her and she didn't like the fact he seemed to see everything going on inside her at a glance.

Scott's intense need to talk was fading. The fact he was simply with her again was changing his agenda. "Have you had lunch yet, Jennifer?"

She grimaced. "Half a bagel while I waited for the prescription to get filled."

He smiled and dropped his coat across one of the kitchen chairs. "Sit. I'll see if you have anything of interest for lunch."

"You don't have to cook for me."

He stopped in front of her and placed his hands gently on her shoulders. "I want to. It makes me feel useful. So just say yes."

"Yes." She leaned forward to place her head against his chest, and his hands closed around her. "I've missed you, Scott. I just don't have the energy to talk right now."

The hands holding her tightened. "Well I'm not letting you shut me out. Got that, Jen? If I have to push my way back in, I'll do so. I don't like you ignoring my calls."

"I'm sorry."

He kissed the top of her head. "You're forgiven. As long as you don't do it again. Now sit while I get to work."

Jennifer sat, her head in her hand, and watched him work. He moved around her kitchen, searching cupboards, looking through the refrigerator, and he soon had lunch underway. Jennifer smiled and watched him.

She had missed him so much. He was big and strong and solid and there, and she loved him so much. She wished things were different, that they had met at a different time in their lives when they would have fit together and not now, when there was destined to be only hurt between them.

Another round of coughing stopped her thinking, and she struggled to regain her breath. Scott brought her a cup of hot tea and rested his hand on her forehead, clearly disturbed that she was sick. Jennifer wanted to lean into his hand. She was simply so weary. She wanted to curl up and go to sleep for hours. She pulled back, causing him to frown. She had been sick before in the last three years, it was just a bad cold, no big deal. It was weakness to lean on Scott after having told him the relationship could go no further.

Scott brought over lunch—soup, salad and fresh fruit.

"Thank you. This looks delicious," Jennifer said, doing her best to do the meal justice. "You took today off from work," she suddenly realized.

"Yes."

She closed her eyes, obviously in pain. "I didn't intend this, Scott. I should have called you."

"I still would have come," he replied. "I can tell you're feeling rotten. Do you want to go lie down for a while or could we talk?"

"There's nothing left to talk about, Scott."

"Yes there is. I love you, Jen, and you love me," he said with quiet confidence, and her eyes filled with tears.

"Well sometimes pain comes with love," she replied.

"I'm not letting you go, Jen."

"You need a wife who can give you a family," she replied, destroying her own hope for his sake.

"I need you."

"And if I can't accept that? What then?"

"I can out-wait you, Jen. Eventually your pain is going to fade to the point you can risk a second marriage."

"I won't let you give up your dream, Scott. You'll resent me for the rest of our lives, and I don't need the extra guilt to carry."

Scott sighed. "Don't sell us short, Jen. Would you rather I stay single for the rest of my life? That's what you're really asking me to do."

* * *

"You shouldn't be outside with your cold."

Jennifer turned on her heels to see Scott approaching.

"Peter told me where you would be," Scott said, not liking at all the puffy eyes and pale face he saw. Jennifer looked awful. He had been trying to reach her last night and this morning with no answer, just the voice of her machine saying to leave a message. She had asked both him and Peter to let her spend this day alone, but Scott couldn't honor that request. She needed someone with her on this day. He needed to be with her today.

There was nothing at the cemetery to block the wind, and it was bitterly cold for mid-December. Scott came to a stop beside Jennifer, looked with pain down at the two headstones on the grave site. He set the bouquet of peach roses he carried down on Colleen's grave. He wanted to take Jennifer's hand, offer some comfort, but she had both hands shoved in her pockets, her expression filled with pain as she looked not at the present but at the past.

When she still stood motionless some minutes later, Scott grew concerned enough he reached out his hand and gently brushed her cheek. His heart was breaking at the pain she was experiencing. "Jen, can you tell me what you're thinking about?"

Jennifer was remembering a previous conversation with Scott.

"I wish I had a picture of Colleen with me so I could show it to you. She had such vivid blue eyes. She used to tilt her head just this certain way and look at you. Then smile.

"She was so tiny when she was born it was a struggle for her to be awake. It took all her energy. So she would lay there and blink at me with this surprised expression in her eyes. They

had to feed her through patches on her back for the first two weeks. It was such a wonderful day when she began to suck."

"What do you miss the most, Jennifer?"

"The fact my life doesn't revolve around her anymore. She gave me a reason to get up every morning. Even if the routine consisted of going to the hospital for the day and sitting with her, she was there. It was devastating after she died not to have her there. I had grown so attached."

"Do you think about having other children, Jennifer?"

"No. Colleen was such a traumatic experience it is going to take a long time for the intensity of those memories to fade. I couldn't risk going through that again."

"You loved Colleen. You would love another child with the same intensity."

"In my mind will always be the fact I lost my eldest daughter."

"Scott, why did she have to die? She was so small, so tiny, she had her whole life ahead of her. It wasn't fair that she died."

Scott wrapped his arms around her and simply hugged her. "I know it wasn't fair, Jen."

"I killed her." Scott felt something cut into his heart at those words. "If I'd only taken better care of myself, she wouldn't have been born early," Jennifer sobbed.

Scott tightened his grip. He couldn't take away the guilt Jennifer was feeling. "Jen, Peter told me a lot about those weeks. You held on long enough to give Colleen life. That was a miracle itself. Your doctors never expected you to make it as long as you did, did Peter ever tell you that? When your blood pressure dropped the doctors were sure you were going to lose the baby. But you didn't. Colleen lived because you held on. Please don't feel this added guilt."

She was crying against his coat, and Scott was helpless to stop her pain. He let her cry and gently rocked her and read the two gravestones over and over.

"You need to get out of this wind," he whispered gently when her tears began to lessen. "Would you come with me? Peter and I will come back for your car."

She nodded, not lifting her head.

Scott walked her back to his car, carefully tucked her into the passenger seat. He turned the heat in the car on full blast and took a few extra minutes to rub her frozen hands. Because she was flushed he lifted his hand to brush her forehead and found she was hot, running at least a hundred-and-one temperature. "Have you eaten today?" he asked gently, tipping her chin up so he could see her eyes.

She shook her head. Scott wasn't surprised.

He called her brother from the car and told him Jennifer was going to be at his place. Jennifer, beside him, barely indicated that she heard the conversation. She rested her head back against the seat and closed her eyes.

Scott looked over at her as he drove. He was convinced she had lost at least ten pounds since that awful day when she had said a definite no to having children. She was giving up hope. Finding her at Colleen's grave today didn't surprise him, but it did worry him. She had no equilibrium about her when she thought about Colleen. She had adjusted to, even accepted Jerry's death. She hadn't done the same with Colleen. She hadn't been able to let go of the trauma. But her comment at the cemetery was at least a clue why. She believed her actions had killed Colleen. Lord, what am I suppose to do? How do I best help her?

She was asleep when Scott pulled into the drive of his house. He didn't wake her. He unlocked the house, propped the door open and gently carried Jennifer inside and laid her carefully down on the couch. He found an afghan his mother had made to cover her with and then he went to the kitchen to fix something she might be able to eat. She needed to take something for the fever, but he would have to wake her to find out what she had taken, and Scott decided the sleep was more important.

He fixed potato soup and toasted bagels for their lunch, carried the food into the living room. "Jen." He shook her shoulder gently. She came awake, groggy, confused. "I brought you some aspirin for the fever. Have you taken anything recently?" Scott asked.

Jennifer struggled to think, lifted the cover back with a hand that felt too heavy to move. "No. Not since early this morning." Scott handed her the aspirins and she swallowed the pills. The lunch smelled so good, and her head, her eyes, hurt so badly.

Scott sat down beside her on the couch, gently brushed back her hair. "Do you want to try to eat?" he asked quietly.

Jennifer closed her eyes, relishing his touch, having missed him so much in the last several days. "In a minute," she replied softly. She opened her eyes a short time later, looked at him with such sadness in her eyes. "Thank you for coming today. I told you not to come, but I was wrong. It was hard to be there alone."

"I'll always be there for you, Jen, please remember that. I'm not going away." Scott could tell she wanted to argue the point, argue that he needed to go away, but the cold was too strong, and she didn't have the strength left to fight. "Try some of the soup," he said, helping her sit up. He sat beside her as she ate, finishing off his own bowl of soup in a fraction of the time it took Jennifer to eat a few bites. When she had eaten all she could, he turned her sidewise on the couch and pulled her to rest back against his chest, and he wrapped the afghan around her and simply held her. He wanted to talk, to ask questions and hear answers and work out a way to heal the pain, but it was not the right time, and there would be a right time; he had to believe that. He held her and let the warmth of his arms help fight the chills that still occasionally rippled through her. "I've missed you," he said gently.

"I've missed you, too." Scott was incredibly pleased to hear those soft words. Jennifer fell asleep in his arms.

Scott was content to simply sit and hold her. When Quigley came looking for them, Scott quietly directed the puppy to come curl up in Jennifer's lap. She woke enough to hug the puppy and drift back to sleep with him snuggled in her arms.

It was harder than last time to convince Jennifer to take a guest bedroom and get some real sleep. She had no intention of staying overnight, and Scott had no intention of letting her be home alone. He gave her the option of staying with Peter and Rachel, or staying with his sister, but he refused to consider letting her be home alone. With Peter backing him up, Scott was finally able to convince her to take a guest room for the night. He put her to bed with a drink on the nightstand beside her, aspirins she could take later that night and extra blankets to keep her from getting chilled.

Scott stood on the landing after finally saying good-night to his guest, and he had to smile. Jennifer was not a good patient.

She slept through breakfast the next morning. Scott was reading the paper around ten when Jennifer finally appeared in the kitchen. Scott wished he could say she looked better, but the fever had done a severe number on her appearance. He didn't care. At least she was up and walking. "Good morning," he said gently, getting up from the table to meet her.

"Is there coffee fixed?" she asked, her voice husky.

"Yes. I'll get it. Take a seat, Jen."

She sat down, weary beyond comprehension.

"How's the fever?"

"Coming down," she said, resting her chin in her hand. "I hate being sick."

"No one enjoys it," Scott replied, setting a cup of coffee and a slice from an apple danish in front of her. "Have you taken more aspirin?" She nodded, and he resumed his seat.

"You took another day off work for me."

He smiled. "I've earned it," he replied. "Jen, would you like to check out my library collection, find a book to read, or would you rather curl up and watch some television? I have several movies on tape," Scott offered.

Jennifer smiled. "Your care is appreciated, but I need to get home."

It was one of the few times he lost a debate with her. She wanted to go home, and he could not dissuade her.

It was hard for Scott to take her home and leave her there. They had to get married soon. He was tired of this.

"Jen, could I ask you a couple of questions?" Scott's breath fluttered some strands of her hair as his voice broke the silence of the room.

They were on the couch in her living room, his arms around her. She was resting back against his chest, her head against his shoulder, a quilt covering her legs. His arms were wrapped firmly around her waist and his hands were comfortably folded atop the quilt with her hands linked under his. The pneumonia had taken her strength, and although her fever was gone, he had no intention of allowing her to move very far.

It was time.

"If I can," she finally said. He heard the hesitation and offered a reassuring kiss across her forehead, and his arms tightened gently. "I've been praying a lot about what has happened, and I just need to understand some things. You might not even know the answers, and that's okay, because that would also help me understand."

She nodded and he felt her take a deep breath. "What're your questions?"

Lord, I could use some help here, Scott prayed.

"I want to know what you are afraid of, specifically. What is it that triggers the terror. Does the thought of being pregnant again make you feel afraid?" He kept his voice calm and steady, and he actually felt some of the stress in her body begin to lessen when he asked the question.

"No. The nausea is hard to handle, but being pregnant was okay."

"Does the memory of giving birth make you afraid?"

He felt the flinch. Okay. That was one answer he needed to know. "What about the memory makes you afraid? The pain? The hospital setting? The doctors?"

Her hands fluttered under his. "It wasn't supposed to be happening, it was too early, I knew I was losing my baby."

Scott turned her hands over to interlace his fingers with hers. She feared another premature birth.

"What if you had a healthy baby like Mary Elizabeth. Does that make you feel afraid?"

He almost thought she had not heard the question she was silent for so long, and then he felt her nod. "She might stop breathing," Jennifer whispered.

SIDS. That one had been obvious. That one should not have been asked.

"If she's four, like Amy, does that make you feel afraid?" he asked, trying to pull that image of an infant from her mind.

Her hands eventually fluttered in his, signaling she didn't know how to answer.

"What about nine like Greg, or twelve, like Tiffany?"

She smiled slightly. "They feel like sturdy kids. Like maybe the worst would be a broken arm."

All right. He had his answers. Scott kissed her forehead and took a deep breath. "Just one last question. If the issue of children were not on the table, is a second marriage itself a problem? Does the idea of being married again make you afraid?"

"I won't rob you of your desire to have a family." It was a flat refusal and he was hurt, because it told him there was going to be quite a fight ahead.

"Does the idea of being married again make you feel afraid?" he asked again, determined to know that basic answer. He gave her time to think about it, and he felt the physical reaction in her body when she finally resolved the question in her mind. His eyes closed. He knew what was coming before she spoke, and it was the answer he had been afraid of the most. In all the pain about Colleen, she sometimes forgot the fact that unexpected death had also claimed Jerry. He had separated them intentionally, suspecting the truth. When she finally spoke, her words were barely a whisper, and they seemed to come as a shock to her. "Yes. The idea of being married again makes me feel terrified."

Chapter Thirteen

Jennifer tried to think through the stroke before she hit the cue ball, but her concentration was simply not there, and as the smooth wood slipped through her fingers and connected with the cue ball she shut her eyes and grimaced. She didn't even have to look to know that her finesse of the eleven ball had instead just left Bob Volishburg an open, easy shot for the game. Her friend called the corner for the eight ball and won the third game with ease.

"You want to tell me what's wrong?" he asked as he watched her pick up the triangle rack and place the balls inside.

I'm terrified of losing another husband so I'm going to walk away from a guy I love. Her face tightened at the awful place she was in. "Not really."

"Tell me, anyway," Bob replied.

Jennifer shook her head and broke the balls apart with a

snap to start their fourth game. Bob had shown up about 10:00 p.m. and offered to play a couple of games. Before that she had simply been lining the balls up in a row and methodically nailing them into the pockets.

"Peter tells me you've been seeing a guy."

"My brother talks too much."

"Well, since I haven't seen you here in three weeks, I'm going to guess it's pretty serious."

"It was," Jennifer agreed.

"Ahh, was. Such an interesting word."

Jennifer smiled grimly. "Not interested."

"You expect me to tell you about Linda, you had better expect me to return the favor," Bob replied. "Jerry wouldn't mind you getting serious with a guy."

"I don't want to lose a husband again," Jennifer said, crushing the ten ball with an explosive shot that sent both it and the cue ball into the side pocket.

Bob placed the penalty ball and considered where he wanted to place the cue ball. "I imagine it's worse than losing a partner," he replied.

Bob had lost two during his career, and Jennifer knew what it had cost him. "It's bad," she agreed. Goodness knows Bob had played her a lot of pool late at night when she was avoiding going home.

"If you've got courage, you'll risk it again. You know what the worst is like."

She was grateful he didn't use the "it's unlikely to happen again" argument. It was an irrelevant argument, and they both knew it. "I don't have that kind of courage. I lost part of myself when I lost Jerry. If I let someone get inside again and I lose him, there won't be much of me left."

"The more rewarding parts of life are risky. You've never been one to play it safe. You don't play it safe when you play pool, you don't play it safe in your writing. You certainly didn't play it safe in how you loved Colleen. But you wouldn't be who you are unless you did take those risks."

"Sometimes you have to pause and count the costs. You did when you left drug enforcement for homicide," Jennifer countered.

Bob shrugged. "I got tired of being shot at. Sure, it's healthy to reconsider the risks you are taking occasionally. But cutting yourself off from risk completely would leave you with a boring life." He smiled. "The last thing either of us can tolerate is boredom."

Jennifer smiled and nailed a ball into the corner pocket. "Maybe I'm getting old, Bob, but it's not as simple as it used to be. I don't want to get hurt again."

"And it's not going to hurt if you walk away?" Bob asked, going to the heart of the matter.

They could adopt. An older child, because Jennifer was going to panic with a child under ten, but adoption was still an option.

Scott tried to weigh what he thought about the idea as he walked the beach with Quigley. He had no rose-colored glasses about the idea. He had met Kevin's friends from foster care. Most of the kids were like Kevin. And while he honestly did like the boy, there was no hiding the fact the kid was troubled and a challenge. Any kid coming out of the system at that age was going to make Jennifer's scars look like paper cuts. Jennifer dealt with her pain remarkably well. A child, without the coping skills of an adult, would be a tangle of anger and pain and nearly impossible to get close to. They would hear "I love you" and likely remember a dozen people in their lives who had said it and then abused or abandoned them. They were kids who desperately needed love and someone to believe in them but who had been hurt so badly in the past they would reject the very thing they most needed to accept. They would likely be in trouble at school, with the law, make discipline and rules a constant battle while they processed the past pain.

She wouldn't marry him if she thought it meant him sacrificing his dreams of a family. The bottom line was that simple. Either she accepted the idea of adoption, or he was going to lose her, Scott understood that. She was serious about not marrying him at the cost of his dream. But to succeed in convincing her to accept adoption, he was going to have to be fully at the point where *he* could accept it. He wasn't going to be able to slide past the reality of what it would mean to adopt an older child and say lightly that it was okay. She would never buy that. He had to believe it was an acceptable solution before he could sell it to her. He couldn't have a doubt left inside.

Could he accept Kevin as his son? Mixed-up, angry, pushing-the-limits Kevin? They would probably have a child very similar to him to deal with. Scott felt the part of him that weighed risks look at and accept the risk. Putting a kid like that back together and through college and out into the world making his own way would be a profound accomplishment. One that was worth the cost.

His biggest fear was over the strain that would put on the marriage. Could they get to the point where they had a strong enough marriage to absorb the stress a child in that shape would cause? It wouldn't be easy dealing with anger and pain coming at them, not because they as parents deserved it but because something in the kid's past was finally getting expressed and they happened to be handy to take the fallout.

Scott called Quigley back to his side and bent down to pick up the puppy.

Lord, what do you want me to do? Are you really setting me up to be adopting older children? Is that what you have planned? I don't want to lose Jennifer. I don't. And if this is the only option, get me to the point I can accept it. Please.

Jennifer's fear of losing a husband was deep and going to be difficult to deal with, but Scott looked at that problem and knew it could be overcome. Adopting an older child; that was different. He had to get not only Jennifer to accept the idea, he had to first reach the point he could honestly accept the idea himself. At the moment, it still left his gut churning with doubt.

"Which ring are you looking at?" Heather asked as she gently rocked Mary Elizabeth back and forth in her arms. Her daughter was awake now and gurgling with delight as she wove her hands into Heather's hair. She and Scott had been walking the mall pushing the infant in her stroller as she slept, shopping for Christmas presents. This was the third time Scott had maneuvered them past this jewelry store.

Scott pointed to the back of the display case. "That one with the center diamond and the offset emerald. The engagement ring has another diamond and an offset ruby. Think she might like it?"

"She'll love it," she replied, getting to the heart of the matter. Jennifer would probably protest the expense, but she would love the ring. She watched her brother sigh and rub the back of his neck. "What's wrong?" Heather asked. Her brother rarely looked this troubled about life, and he'd had to work at showing an interest in Christmas shopping and that was not like him. He shrugged and didn't answer. As it now seemed likely that he was not going to be buying the rings today, Heather gently tugged his arm. "Come on, let's go eat lunch."

They went to a sandwich and soup shop on the lower level of the mall, slid into a booth. Their sandwiches and soup arrived and Scott smiled at how active Mary Elizabeth was. "Hand her to me, Twig, while you eat your soup," Scott offered, and his sister handed him the baby. "Hey, M, how you doing today? You like all these colors and lights, don't you? Are you going to like to shop like your mom does?" The infant smiled and gurgled and threw her arms up at him, her legs pushing against his thighs. Scott laughed and kissed her cheek. He settled her against his shoulder and looked over at his sister. His eyes were grave.

"We're not going to have children. She's so afraid, Twiggy." There were tears in his eyes that he didn't let fall.

Her hand covered his. "I'm so sorry, Scott."

He hesitated. *Twig, it hurts so bad.* "So am I," he finally said. It was his pain to cope with.

"You can borrow Mary Elizabeth anytime you like. The kids love having you as their uncle," she said, trying to help.

"Thanks, Twig. I'm going to do that."

"After lunch, go buy the rings, Scott," Heather told him, knowing that decision was the only one that was going to give him some peace.

"You really think she would like those rings?" he asked, fighting back the pain.

Heather couldn't remember her brother ever being this uncertain. "Absolutely. Those rings are gorgeous," she reassured him, smiling.

"I found a gold band that I like, too."

"Come on in, Scott. Sorry I'm running late," Jennifer called from the kitchen.

Scott pushed open the door and stepped inside, shaking the light dusting of snow from the coat he'd taken off and carrying it into the kitchen with him. He dropped it over the back of a chair. The house was festive and colorful and Jennifer had Christmas music playing. "How did the cookies turn out?"

Jennifer smiled at him from the counter where she was boxing the iced cookies. "They turned out great. Tiffany, Tom and Alexander all approved."

Scott came over and rested his hands against her back, leaned over to kiss her. Her peach sweater felt soft and warm against his hand, and he rubbed her back softly. "There's no hurry. I told Mom we'd be by sometime this evening to drop the boxes off, but they aren't due to the nursing home until tomorrow afternoon. I think the youth group managed to make twenty dozen total, I picked up the last of them on the way over."

Jennifer paused in her work. "I'm glad your mom does this. I don't bake cookies if it's just for me. And there are only so many I can pass on to Peter and Rachel and the kids."

"Which are the best? The Christmas trees, the reindeer or the candy canes?" Scott asked, studying the options.

"Try a candy cane. They break so easily when they're packed."

Scott picked up one and found the sugar cookie was delicious. "You haven't eaten yet have you?" he asked, hoping she had been willing to wait.

"I had a late lunch. Where do you have in mind? I'll need to change."

"The jeans are fine. I thought we would go split a sample plate at Shaw's," he offered.

"Sounds wonderful." She finished boxing the last cookies and added the box to the stack on the table. Her hands finally free, she came back to hug him. "How are you tonight?" she asked quietly.

He settled his hands around her waist and tucked her close. He liked the feel of her hands on his back. He kissed her leisurely. "I'm doing fine. I've missed you the past couple days," he said, studying her brown eyes, which reminded him so much of a young doe. She had beautiful eyes.

She sighed and leaned her head against his chest, and he took the opportunity to gently rub her shoulders and the back of her neck. He could feel the tension in her body. "I'm so glad you're around. I really don't like Christmas, and that's an awful feeling."

He rubbed her back, long soothing strokes across her shoulders and spine down to her waist. "I know." She had not been able to hide the sadness in her eyes, and he knew the memories were there and bothering her. "We'll keep you too busy to think about it. We're going to Rachel and Peter's for Christmas Eve?"

"If you're sure you want to. You ought to spend it with your own family."

Her protest caused him to smile. "You're going to be my family," he replied lightly.

"Scott..."

He tipped her chin up and kissed her before she could protest any further. "We'll go to my folks for lunch Christmas Day," he said. He nodded toward the boxes on the table. "It's cold outside. You'll need your long coat," he recommended.

She wanted the conversation to continue, he could see that, but after she looked at him she dropped her eyes and simply nodded. Scott squeezed her hands gently before he let her go. He was going to ask her tonight. He'd just made that decision.

Scott didn't have to persuade Jennifer very hard to get her to slide over on the seat and sit beside him on the drive to his parents'. He entwined his hand with hers as it rested on the seat. She was lost in thought, and Scott didn't try to break it. It felt right, having her with him, and it was so different from that night a couple months before as he had driven alone to his parents' for his birthday party. It was nice having her with him. His mom was home but not his dad, and Scott didn't linger at their place. He and Jennifer carried the boxes she had packed and those from the youth group into the dining room, where his Mom had several other donations packed. Scott kissed his Mom at the door and could see the question in her eyes, and he just smiled. He never had been able to keep a secret from her, and she knew something was different tonight. "We'll see you for lunch Christmas Day," he told her, giving her a hug.

Jennifer thought the restaurant would be packed with holiday gatherings, but the parking lot at the seafood restaurant was only partially full. Scott got out and came around to open her door, offer his arm across the slick parking lot. They were seated at a back booth of the restaurant and Scott ordered a large sample plate and two diet colas for them. "Is your Christmas shopping done?" Scott asked her as they both selected a freshly baked bread stick from the basket the waitress had brought.

She grinned. "Rachel's gift was the last one I needed, and I got that this morning. Did you find Heather's gift?"

Scott smiled. "I bought her an orchid. One plant that is flowering and several bulbs that she can plant."

"She'll love it."

Scott went silent for several minutes. "You're really missing Colleen, aren't you?" he asked quietly.

Jennifer wished he could not read the pain so easily. "Incredibly. She never got to see a Christmas," Jennifer sighed and wished there was some way to make the pain go away. "Most of the nursery was packed away shortly after Colleen died—the crib, the changing table. But I've still got the rocking chair, the clothes I made for her, the ankle ID band she wore. I keep telling myself I'm going to pack them away and turn the bedroom back into a guest room, but when I go in the room all I want to do is rock in the chair and cry." She felt so miserable admitting that.

"Jen, maybe that's what you need to do the most. Let yourself cry."

"I've cried enough, Scott."

His hand gently rubbed the back of hers. She had to force herself not to turn her hand into his and hold on. "You lost a lot, Jen. Allow yourself the freedom to grieve."

His concern and kindness was almost too much to take. "Could we talk about something else?" she asked, hoping he would not be offended.

He smiled.

"Tell me about your book," he offered. The sample plate of seafood arrived and they talked about her book over steamed scallops, garlic shrimp, mussels on the shell, and Louisiana blue crab claws. Jennifer felt the sadness inside lift as she sat talking with Scott. She loved him. It went as deep as it had with Jerry, and she wished so badly she could get past the terror of having children so they could have a future together. But she was resolute that she would do what was best for him, and right now, it was not her. But Bob was right. It was going to hurt so very, very badly to walk away.

They left the restaurant shortly after 8:00 p.m., and when Scott suggested they go for a drive, Jennifer gladly agreed. When she was with him, the pain was less.

Scott looked over at Jennifer as he drove, wishing he had some idea how she was going to respond to his proposal. There were times in his life when he put his heart into someone else's hands, and tonight was going to be one of them.

"Jen?"

She turned toward him and smiled, and it reached her eyes and made her so beautiful. "Yes?"

"Slide over here," he encouraged.

She slid over with a smile and his arm settled around her shoulders. "Where are we going?"

Scott smiled. "How does a fire, a cup of hot chocolate and a very enthusiastic puppy sound?"

"Delightful."

Quigley greeted her at the door with a cold nose and a squirming body. Jennifer scooped him up with a laugh after handing Scott her coat. "Hello, Quigley, my little beautiful boy." The puppy licked her chin and Jennifer laughed, and when she rubbed his ears he squirmed closer with a happy wiggle.

"Take him into the living room. I'll be right in with the hot chocolate. The fire is already laid and ready to start," Scott said as he rested his hand against her back and lightly ruffled the puppy's fur.

When Scott entered the living room some ten minutes later, the fire had been started and Jennifer had kicked off her shoes and curled up at one end of the couch with Quigley nearly asleep in her arms. Scott settled beside her and carefully handed her one of the mugs he carried. He smiled and ran his finger across the bridge of her foot. "I like the socks."

"Thank you, I thought the Christmas trees were appropriate."

Scott stretched his legs out and leaned his head back, watched the flickering flames surrounding the logs. They sat in silence for several minutes, both enjoying the stillness. Jennifer shifted around so she could rest against his shoulder, and Scott gladly welcomed her into his arms. "What are you thinking about so deeply?" she asked.

Scott took a deep breath. It was time. Lord, help my words be the right ones.

"What would you say to adopting an older child?" he asked quietly, then turned his head to look down at her.

"Adopting?"

"You know I want a family Jen, but I really do understand how terrified you are of the idea of having children again. We could adopt a kid like Kevin." Scott smiled. "He's anything but fragile you know."

"Yes, he is, inside."

Scott gently stroked her hair. "I know you're right. People just forget it occasionally when they bump into that shell of his."

Jen gripped his hand. "You really would consider adopting an older child and all the problems that might bring?"

Scott wished he could read her voice well enough to know if that was hope or fear he heard, but all he could know for sure was that the calm, relaxed lady he had been holding a few moments before was now stiff and tense. His hands rubbed her arms, trying to dispel the tension.

"Jen, you need to be a mother. Having a family is as much your dream as it is mine. That dream didn't disappear when Colleen died, it just got badly battered." He kissed the top of her head. "You will make a good mom. I know that with certainty."

Her eyes were damp as he brushed her hair back from her face. He reached behind her for the gift he had set on the end table. "This is for you," he said quietly, placing both her hands around the small package. He smiled at her expression. "Go ahead, open it," he encouraged.

Her hands shook a little as she removed the ribbon and the deep green wrapping paper. She hesitated before opening the ring box.

"Will you marry me, Jen?"

The tears had begun to fall, and Scott wiped them away, wrapping her in his arms. He slid the engagement ring from the velvet slot and placed it in the palm of her hand. "I like this ring. It's special, just like the one you already wear. We could have something very special too, Jen, if you'll say yes."

Her hand closed around the ring and held it very tightly. "You're proposing and you want us to adopt." There was so much emotion in her voice...

Scott raised her hand and pressed his lips to the back of it. "Yes."

He felt her ragged breath, "I don't know what to say."

"Say you'll think about it," Scott said gently, his hands cupping her face, raising her face to let him fully see her. All the emotion was there in her eyes—the uncertainty, the fear, the love, the hope, the pain. He deliberately smiled, having just put his future and hers on the line. "I'm going to marry you, Jen. We're going to have a family, and we're going to make a difference in each other's lives and in the lives of whatever children God entrusts to us. I love you, Jen."

She buried her head against his chest and fought for her composure. "I'll think about it."

He kissed her forehead. "Think as long as you need to, Jen. I'm not going anywhere," he promised. He'd put it all on the line, and now it was a waiting game.

Chapter Fourteen

Could she adopt? Could she face the fear of being married again, adopt and raise a family? Or was she walking away?

The night was freezing cold, two weeks before Christmas. She couldn't stay out for long, even with the gloves and scarf, but Jennifer felt the need to see the stars, and so she sat on the hammock in the backyard and leaned back and looked up. The stars in the Milky Way were bright and clear. Jennifer sat and looked at the sky and waited for the sense of being part of something enormous to settle into her soul. This decision was important, but it wasn't going to change the course of the universe. It would change her life and Scott's life and to a certain degree the lives of both of their families. She could make this decision. But what was the right decision?

The cold touch of death sat so close; incredible in its intensity. How could she risk getting married again? Even an older child. Could she really be a mom again?

Knowing what she had to do if she was to make a decision, Jennifer walked back inside, took off her coat and gloves, paused to hang them up and walked resolutely past her bedroom. She paused at the door of the nursery, took a deep breath and turned the handle. It was so quiet in the room, with a very faint scent of lavender from the dried flower display on the dresser. Walking slowly into the place she considered to be the heart of her home, she gently lifted from the dresser the clothes she had made for Colleen to wear, nightshirts and jumpers and very small socks. She smiled as she touched the soft fabric, remembering the love that had gone into making the garments, laughed as she remembered the sewing lessons Rachel had given her and how difficult it had been to make her fingers create what her mind envisioned. She took the garments with her and sat down in the rocking chair, smoothing them out with care on the leg of her jeans. She refused to let the tears fall. There was pain here, deep pain. So many dreams had ended so abruptly.

Jennifer very carefully folded the clothes, leaned her head back and closed her eyes. For the first time in recent days she let herself go back in time to the funerals, and actually think about what the experiences had been like. The first images that hit her were the coffins, polished oak, the wood grains deep and smooth. She had requested peach roses for Colleen's coffin, deep red roses for Jerry's coffin, and the flowers had rested on the center of the coffins, paying tribute to the memories she had of each. She felt and heard the music, felt the support of those standing with her, felt such a great distance from her God. In three years she had passed through the anger and despair—she now had a gentle peace with her God—but the taste of death still lingered. She couldn't lose Scott the same way. She couldn't. She would never survive.

It was time to accept reality.
The fear had won.

Scott dressed slowly, taking time to fasten his cuff links, choose the right tie, polish his shoes. He knew he was deliberately delaying the time he would leave his home to pick up Jennifer, even found himself amused at his actions, but did nothing to speed up his movements. He didn't know which way she was going to decide, but he was determined to hear her answer with as much dignity as he could. He'd either won or he'd lost for good. Either way, there would only be gratitude in his heart tonight for having known her. He loved her. He had placed her in the toughest position of her life, asking her to face her fear, without him being there to provide support. He picked up the single rose Heather had picked for him to give to Jennifer, a special rose—pale pink and white, perfectly formed.

Have courage, Jen. Please, have courage.

It was Christmas Eve and the music on the radio reflected the Christmas season. Scott drove slowly, carefully, eventually pulled into her subdivision, then her street, and finally into her drive. He parked the car, picked up the rose to shelter it from the wind and walked to her front door. She answered within moments of him ringing the bell and he smiled when he saw her. She was dressed for the Christmas Eve services, as well, her dress a wonderful deep blue velvet with satin trim. He kissed her cheek softly, and she hugged him, but there was nothing he could read in her eyes.

"Can we talk after we leave Peter and Rachel's?" she asked quietly, and he forced himself to take a deep breath. She wouldn't be so hesitant to share good news.

"Of course, Jen," he said quietly, wanting nothing more than to hold her tight and not let her go. But he owed her for adding a richness to his life he would have found nowhere else; he wasn't going to make the evening any harder on her than it was already destined to be. "I brought this for you," he said gently, pressing the rose into her hand.

She lifted the rose to smell its fragrance, touched the delicate pedals with the tips of her fingers. She lifted her eyes from the rose, an enormous sadness in those brown eyes, and she reached up and gently kissed him. "Thank you," she whispered.

He did hug her then, pulling her tight and simply holding her, and she clung to him in return, and minutes passed before she stepped away. "Let me put this in water."

He could see her reaching for strength deep inside, hear it in her voice. "I'll get your coat for you," he said, and she nodded and turned away. When she came back from the kitchen, the sadness in her eyes had been buried and replaced by calm acceptance. She slipped into her coat and pulled on her gloves. "I'm ready," she said quietly.

He locked the house for her, offered her his arm for the slick pavement, opened the passenger door. It was a silent drive to the area church Christmas Eve gathering. They both knew their respective families would be present at the area church gathering, but silently agreed not to seek out either friends or family. They sat together during the service, Scott firmly holding Jennifer's hand the entire time, and when the service was over, they slipped quietly back through the crowds. They waited for most of the parking lot to clear before Scott pulled from the church lot and asked Jennifer for directions.

Peter and Rachel's house was adorned with Christmas lights. Some were in the evergreens, others on the porch railing, some outlining windows. Jennifer drew a deep breath as they neared the front door, knowing that they would be expected and quickly pulled into the festivities, and knowing as well that she badly needed time to gather herself for the discussion later with Scott. Peter and Scott shook hands, and Rachel and Jennifer shared a hug. Jennifer didn't let her friend go for some time. "You okay?" Rachel whispered, and Jennifer nodded. Scott and Jennifer were escorted to the love seat in the living room, across from the Christmas tree and the presents the children had selected to be opened that night. There was cider and cheese and sausage, crackers, Christmas cookies. The boys gravitated to Scott, eager to have his attention. They made Scott smile, and Jennifer was grateful. She wished so badly the evening could end some other way. Scott reached over and put his arm around her shoulders, gently pulling her to his side. She looked up, surprised, and he tenderly brushed the hair back from her face and smiled. She could see the sadness in his eyes, but also a love so great that he would still offer comfort. She wished she could offer the same comfort in return.

As the evening progressed, Jennifer let herself relax and enjoy the time with her family. The children so enjoyed the celebration. The memories of past Christmas Eves spent with Jerry and her family returned, and they were good memories.

She couldn't give Scott up. She loved him. He had just split a sugar cookie and offered her half of it with a smile. She loved him. She couldn't give him up. She'd come with a heavy heart tonight knowing she couldn't accept the risk of facing death again, had to say goodbye, but she couldn't carry out the sentence. She loved him. She was going to have to find a way to take the risk.

He knew something had changed. He held her gaze without wavering, his arm around her shoulder tightened, and he gently leaned over and kissed her.

They left Peter and Rachel's shortly after ten. Jennifer leaned her head back as they walked to the car; the sky was clear and bright with stars. Her hand was tucked firmly in Scott's, and it felt so right. "Where would you like to go?" he asked quietly.

Jennifer looked at the man she loved and quietly replied, "The beach, where we first met."

There was no wind, the water was calm, and the sand shifted as they walked. Scott had picked up both a quilt and a blanket at the house, and he spread the quilt out on the pier steps, helping her take a seat. He tucked the blanket around her legs. "Warm enough?" he asked, placing an arm around her shoulders and her coat. She smiled and slid another inch toward him. "I'm fine."

She didn't say anything for several minutes, her attention focused on the water and the starlit sky. "I was going to tell you *no.*"

She felt his tension, and she could hear his deep, controlled breathing. "And now?" he asked softly.

She leaned her head against his shoulder. "I'm petrified of losing you, but I'll marry you." He laughed at the way she worded her acceptance, hugging her close. "I love you too much to say goodbye," she said.

He tilted her head up with both of his hands, his touch gentle, love in his eyes. "Jen, you won't regret this." Jennifer slipped her hands around his neck, gently moved them up into his silky hair. It was a deep kiss, full of love on both sides. "You are the very best thing that ever happened to me," he whispered, soothing away the lingering fear in her eyes with hands that gently stroked her face. "I'll help keep the fear away. You'll make it, honey, love can do it."

"The idea of adopting older kids...it doesn't feel too bad," she said, smiling slightly as she tugged his skewed tie straight again.

"Really?" His smile was delightful to see.

"Really," she confirmed.

He settled his arms around her waist under her coat, rested his forehead against hers. "How many children would you like?" he asked, interested.

She smiled. "Two or three would be nice."

His arms tightened. "Thank you, Jen."

She kissed him.

He got pragmatic. "Jen, I hate to disturb this moment, but it's cold out here. Let's go find your purse. I want to put that ring on your finger."

She laughed. He tugged her to her feet and picked up the blankets, escorted her inside. She found her purse and removed the ring box, handed it to him. He laughed softly at the way her hands were suddenly trembling, held them in his until they steadied.

"Important moment, isn't it?" he asked, breaking the tension.

She laughed, then, and relaxed. "It's big," she agreed. She moved the wedding ring she wore to her right hand and touched it, remembering. He gave her time, and she appreciated that. "Okay," she said quietly.

Scott gently slipped the engagement ring on her finger, smiled and kissed the back of her hand. "It looks good there." She hugged him, and he closed his arms around her to hold her tight. "Let's call Peter and Rachel. We'll tell my family tomorrow."

Neither Scott nor Jennifer minded the long drive to his parents' home. It was a chance to share the enjoyment of the moment. Jennifer sat close to Scott as he drove, her hand tucked in his.

"Marry me soon," Scott said over the Christmas music. He looked over at her, smiled. He'd read her fear correctly. She didn't need time to question her decision. It didn't matter what his friends and family thought. The wedding needed to be soon. When she didn't respond, he looked over again. Her brown eyes were calm and clear and slightly wet. "Bad idea or good?"

"Good one," she breathed. "Could we elope?"

He laughed. "No. Mom would kill me. How about thirty days? Third Saturday in January?"

Jennifer didn't have to think about it. "Yes."

Scott grinned. He could wait thirty days. Maybe.

His family was waiting for them to arrive, and when they pulled into the drive, Amy and Greg both came out to meet them, bundled up in coats and mittens. "Hi, Uncle Scott." Scott picked Amy up with a laugh and tickled her. He ruffled the boy's hair.

"Hi, Greg. Is lunch ready?"

"We were waiting for you," Greg replied.

"Then let's get inside," he agreed. He caught Jennifer's hand as they walked up the porch steps, shared a private smile with her.

It was his mother who first noticed the ring. Jennifer was taking off her coat and handing it to Scott's father when Margaret caught her breath and immediately looked over Jennifer's shoulder to Scott. He smiled and linked his arms around Jennifer's shoulders.

"Mom, Dad, we've got some news." He didn't have to say more, his smile said it all. Jennifer was swept into a hug by his mother who was now laughing and wiping away tears, his father was hugging him, and both Heather and Frank were crowding into the entryway to celebrate the news. The kids were thrilled, their eyes sparkling with excitement.

The family was sitting down to lunch when Scott paused behind Jennifer's chair, put his hands on her shoulders and looked around at his family. "We are getting married the third Saturday in January." Surprise, shock, bewilderment, he saw them all on their faces. He smiled. "This decision is right for us. But we could use your help, there are details to sort out."

Within an hour of the Christmas lunch announcement, Rachel and Peter and the kids had been invited over to make it a family celebration. Scott sat on the couch with Jennifer, watching his sister and mom tossing wedding details back and forth with Rachel. This felt right. This felt perfect. Their two families meshed so well. Jennifer had chosen colors for the dresses, and the wedding party had been decided on; they were working on the reception plans now.

From where he was sitting Scott could see Quigley trying to wrestle a tennis shoe underneath the great blue spruce in the foyer. Too tall and massive to fit in any conventional room, the Christmas tree towered in the curve of the stairway, reaching toward the skylight. He and Jennifer had helped decorate it, a process that involved leaning over the stair railing to reach the high branches. The gifts were gone now allowing Quigley a place he considered to be his new home, hiding down in the fluffy red-and-white tree skirt under the low branches. Scott saw Tiffany chase him down again, try to convince the puppy not to drink out of the Christmas tree base.

It was tradition in the neighborhood to go Christmas caroling on Christmas Eve, and as twilight came the adults began sorting out coats and gloves. All the kids wanted to go. Neighbors would have hot cider and cookies for the carolers. "Can I ride on your shoulders, Uncle Scott?" Amy asked, tugging at his hand.

"I'm staying here with Jennifer," he replied, and Jennifer saw the disappointment on the little girl's face.

"Go with them, Scott. There's no need for you to stay simply because I'm getting over a bad cold."

"I think the doctor called it pneumonia," he reminded her.

"Mom, aren't you coming?" Greg also looked disappointed.

"Mary Elizabeth is asleep upstairs. I need to stay here," Heather told her son.

They were the only two holdouts, everyone else, including Peter and Rachel were going. "Listen, both of you, go with the kids. I can listen for Mary Elizabeth. She's only been asleep half an hour. She'll never know you were gone," Jennifer insisted. She could see that this was a long-standing tradition, and she knew how much fun it was to go caroling.

"Jen, are you sure?" Heather asked.

"Positive."

She looked at Scott. He reluctantly removed his arm and got up, leaned back down to kiss her. "I was hoping for thirty minutes on our own," he whispered, and she laughed.

She saw everyone off, watched as they joined up with neighbors who were also out to go caroling. She closed the door with a laugh as Quigley tried to sneak through. "No, you don't, friend. You get to keep me company. Tiffany will be back in an hour."

The house was silent with everyone gone. The massive Christmas tree blinked its colored lights, the smell of greenery wonderful. It had been such a beautiful day.

Jennifer went over to the baby monitor and made sure it was turned all the way up. She sat on the couch and played tug of war with Quigley using an old rag someone had found for him. He grew tired of the game after about ten minutes, and Jennifer let him run again. He was going to eventually be one very tired puppy. Smiling, she picked up the glasses and dishes around on the tables and carried them into the kitchen, loading the dishwasher.

Twenty minutes and she had heard nothing from Mary Elizabeth. Jen knew what was driving her desire to check on the infant but went, anyway. She walked up the stairs with Quigley underfoot, quietly pushed open the door of the guest room where Margaret had a crib set up. The baby was sleeping peacefully. Jen watched her breathe, reached out very gently to touch the softness of her little hand. She was so beautiful. So big. So healthy. Jennifer watched her and smiled, quietly left the room.

The kids would be cold when they got back. Finding that Margaret had set out all the ingredients for hot chocolate, Jennifer read her recipe and set to work. She tasted the drink as it heated and knew she was going to have to get a copy. The recipe had a pinch of Dutch chocolate in it. It was delicious.

Quigley yelped. Jennifer tilted her head, trying to figure out where it had come from, but it was not repeated. Not liking the fact he hadn't come bolting back into the kitchen after encountering another dust ball surprise, Jennifer carefully turned down the flame under the large pan heating the hot chocolate and set aside the long spoon. "Quigley? Where are you, boy?"

Jennifer walked through the living room, expecting to find him stuck under one of the couches. The flicker of orange caught the corner of her eye, and she turned. She froze. Flames were licking up the back of the Christmas tree. Smoke was beginning to billow up and fill the stairwell.

The fire alarm went off just as she understood what was happening. The tree was big and dry, and the flames were engulfing it so quickly.

The baby. Quigley, who must be beneath the tree, she had to leave to fend for himself. There wasn't time to call for help. There was only one way upstairs and it would soon be impassable. Covering her nose and mouth with her hands, Jen plowed through the smoke accumulating on the landing and made it to the upper hallway. The smoke was only beginning to collect here. It was still filling into the skylight.

Mary Elizabeth was crying at the piercing noise of the alarm. Jen gathered the infant and all her blankets together, tried to not let her own terror make her hold the baby too tightly. She lightly covered the baby's face with the edge of a blanket to protect her from the smoke. She was not losing another baby. She would claw death in the face before she would let that happen.

The hallway was filling with smoke as she exited the guest room. She kept her head low. She could hear Quigley now, barking in a panic from somewhere downstairs, and she felt the relief. She loved that puppy.

"Hold on, Mary Elizabeth, it's time to see what our exit looks like," Jen told the child, trying to keep low to keep the screaming infant from breathing in smoke. Jen could feel it already burning her eyes and making her stressed lungs choke. She turned the corner and felt the intense heat hit her. The blue spruce was totally engulfed. The edges of the stairway carpet were on fire, and she couldn't see to the bottom of the stairs, the smoke was so thick.

Jen ducked back away from the corner and the heat, choking on the smoke.

There was no other way off this floor but a window. It was the smoke that would kill them. Mary Elizabeth wouldn't be able to survive even a couple of breaths of this acidic smoke. She couldn't drop her from a second floor window. Knowing her options were limited, Jennifer rushed toward the nearest bedroom. There was not a single person on the street. She grabbed the blanket off the foot of the bed and ran to the bathroom. The shower drenched it in seconds and Jennifer didn't waste time shutting the water off. She heard glass shatter. The fire had burst thru the skylight.

The flames now had a vent, and while the air fed the flames, it actually gave Jennifer one great big break. The smoke rushed up, the skylight becoming a large chimney. For the first time she got a look at the entire stairwell. None of the stairs had collapsed, the outer wall was still free of fire, the carpet showing itself surprisingly resistant to the dropping embers. It was melting, Jennifer realized, not burning.

"Mary Elizabeth, I love you," Jen sobbed, kissing the still screaming infant, "please hold your breath." She had to make the front door.

She wanted to run and could only hurry, forced to take the steps at a pace where she would not trip. She held the baby wrapped in the soaked blanket and turned toward the outer wall. The searing heat on her right came right through the wet blanket and drove her almost to her knees as she tried to slide past the burning tree. She was at the landing, and she could see the front door, near, and yet so many steps away. Her lungs stopped drawing air. The smoke combined with the lingering effects of pneumonia was too much to handle. Quigley was having a fit down below, desperate to reach her.

Mary Elizabeth was going to die in her care. Oh, God, no. Not again. Tears flooded her eyes, and she was choking.

She cleared the final step, whimpering at the pain and the desperate need to breathe, Mary Elizabeth tucked and protected in her arms.

God, please help me.

She didn't make it to the front door.

"Look, Uncle Scott. Smoke!" Amy tugged his hair to get his attention. She was perched on his shoulders, looking all around. She had actually tugged his head in the direction of the smoke, and Scott couldn't help but see it.

The girl came tumbling off his shoulders. "Dad, that's Grandma's place!"

There were fifteen adults in the caroling party, all neighbors. They were a block to the west of the house. They were seeing the vent of smoke billowing through the skylight.

"Mary Elizabeth!" Heather screamed.

Frank, Scott and Peter made the block at a dead run, cutting through flower beds and bushes. Flames were coming through the skylight now. There was no sign of Jennifer and the baby. The fire was in the worst part of the house, blocking the stairs, the hallway, all the exits. Scott got to the front door first, scalded his hand on the hot metal only to realize someone must have turned the latch, locking the door when it closed. Frank headed toward the back of the house.

Peter broke out the living room window.

If Jen was upstairs with the baby... Scott forced himself not to think about it. They would never get to them in time. The bedroom window above him blew out, showering them with glass.

Scott followed Peter through the window. The smoke billowing around the room choked him. "There!" Peter screamed to be heard over the deafening roar of the fire. She'd made it past the burning tree and to within touching distance of the front door. The wallpaper and hallway was totally engulfed in flames, the stairwell was gone. The burning tree was threatening to fall in her direction.

Peter scrambled to yank the burning floor rugs away from her face. "Get them out of there!"

Scott dropped to his knees and dove for her, feeling the heat try to burn him alive.

"Mary Elizabeth!"

"Here," Scott yelled to Frank. Jen was curled around the infant.

Scott grabbed the two of them and yanked them clear of the leaning tree. Kneeling, he passed the crying infant to her father. Her cries were a wonderful sound.

The sodden blanket had protected Jen's hair from burning, but she wasn't moving, and she wasn't breathing. "Grab her!" Scott yelled, lifting her toward the window. Peter got through and took her weight, and Scott yanked himself through the window after them.

Peter had her on the driveway, the blanket off and the cinders on her clothes stamped out, but he wasn't getting any air into her lungs. Her blood, no oxygen in it, had turned her skin blue. There was enough medical training present to deal with a trauma victim, but no one could bring the dead back to life.

Scott sat on the cold concrete next to her, held her burned hand and watched his sister do CPR, and Peter trying to get her to breathe, and he started to silently cry.

Chapter Fifteen

"Hi, precious." She would know those blue eyes anywhere. Jennifer held out her arms and Jerry handed her the baby, gurgling and smiling and waving her arms, happy. Colleen hadn't grown, but her eyes were bright, her small body strong. She grinned and flirted with her Mom, bubbling kisses at her, delighted at the long hair she could tug. Jennifer grinned and offered her necklace instead.

There was fire in the dream now, fire between her and her husband, her child, then they were gone.
Mary Elizabeth. No!

God, I can't do this. I can't. Not another child.

"Jennifer!" It was a strong voice that compelled her attention. "You keep fighting, you hear me? Mary Elizabeth is fine. She's home. Do you hear me? Don't you dare give up!"

She was not fighting to live. That was the hardest part for Scott to grasp. She'd been on the respirator five days now, slowly growing worse. But he thought he understood. She had collapsed in a burning house holding a baby, her last conscious thoughts the realization Mary Elizabeth was going to die because she had not made it to the door. Jennifer wouldn't want to live, knowing that. He told her Mary Elizabeth was fine, over and over again, and she heard him, her hand flinched when he spoke to her, but she only got worse. *Please Jen, don't do this. Don't leave.* It was like she didn't believe him. It began to make him mad.

"Jen, I had Rachel reserve the church this morning, and Mom is sending out the wedding invitations. You've got twenty-five days left before your wedding, so I suggest you try fighting this respirator. This give-up attitude is not appreciated."

If one set of tactics did not work, it was time to try a second. Scott watched her hand flinch, knew she could hear him. She had been hearing him for the last five days, but hadn't been willing to fight back to consciousness. Her burns had to hurt, her right hand and arm had blistered, but they were all first degree, they would heal with only minor scars. He had told her that, but nothing was getting her to fight.

Her hand twitched and this time slightly turned.

"You have to open your eyes, Jen. You can't sleep anymore. Open your eyes," he ordered.

She did. She looked annoyed and she closed them again, but she'd opened her eyes.

Scott laughed around his tears. "Oh, no you don't. Get back here. Open your eyes."

They opened again and she blinked at him. It was hard to see a smile around a respirator, but her eyes softened. He gently kissed her forehead. "Mary Elizabeth is fine. You did good, Jen. You did good."

Chapter Sixteen

Jennifer woke early on Saturday morning, her wedding day, the house quiet and still, though it would change in the next hour as Rachel and Beth arrived. Jennifer listened to the peaceful quiet, her last morning in this house, and smiled. She was going to miss this place. She considered burying her head under the pillows again and letting the next hour drift by, but knew she didn't really have that luxury. She flexed her stiff right hand, feeling the tightness in the skin around her fingers that still lingered even after the blisters had healed. The stiffness in her skin, the inhalator she used twice a day, were the only remaining marks of the fire. The doctors told her another month would remove even them. After ten days in the hospital she had been ready to get home. She rose, stretched, slipped on her robe and walked through the house to the kitchen to start coffee. The stress in her system was totally gone, and it made her feel like a new person. Fear had been her companion for three years, and it was gone now. She felt wonderful. Peaceful.

Scott's parents' home had been a total loss, but they seemed to be handling it without too much despair. Jennifer hadn't been back. She didn't want to see the burnt-out shell, and the wrecking crews had come in ten days later. Margaret in particular had taken the loss calmly. They were people who grasped material things lightly, and when they were taken away, those people were not crushed. The picture albums had actually been at Heather's that day, and some of their more precious keepsakes from the master bedroom had been recovered. That was all Margaret considered irreplaceable. They were staying with friends in the neighborhood, planning to rebuild in the spring. Scott had offered them his home, and Jennifer had urged them to accept, goodness knew it was spacious enough, but they had declined. Olivia and Jack had been friends for thirty years and their children were grown, Margaret and Larry were more comfortable staying with them, where they could walk to the site and oversee the construction.

Jennifer drank her coffee standing up, looking out over the front lawn, white now from snow that had come down overnight. They had chosen wedding colors to match the winter season. Beth's and Rachel's gowns were deep green, Scott's and Brad's tuxes were black with deep red accessories; poinsettias would dominate the decorations in the church. Heather, of course, planned to see that the flowers were spectacular. There would be guests, over a hundred had already confirmed, and Heather's friend Tracy was providing the music. Jennifer knew her dress would look spectacular against such a setting. She had done away with the long train and instead gone for simplicity, choosing a white silk classical gown.

Scott had made the honeymoon plans and given her not a single hint of where they were going, only that they would be gone a week. Even the clothes he had suggested she pack gave her no clue. She walked through the house carrying a fresh cup of coffee. There were gifts to wrap. Jennifer smiled at the thought. She went to her office and picked up the packages. She had gifts for the wedding party, but those were already wrapped. The gifts still to be wrapped were for Scott.

It was a little thing, letting him choose what she wore at night, but it was an important gift. A few of the boxes she wrapped were to make that gift possible. The other gifts, they were simply things that would serve as memories for both of them—a copy of a book Ann had helped her get autographed, a sweater she had found for him, an engraved watch. The gifts were small, but they would make a memory, and that was the reason for them.

The gifts were wrapped and Jennifer was putting the final touches to what was packed in her suitcase when Rachel and Beth arrived. Her friends carried breakfast with them, and their excitement made Jennifer smile. Jennifer sat at the kitchen table with them, sharing a raspberry danish and listening as her two friends went through the details for the day. Jennifer put herself in their capable hands—her hair was brushed silky smooth, her makeup was done with an expert hand. When they arrived at the church her dress and veil had been laid out in the dressing room, a room filled with a profusion of flowers from Scott.

She dressed quietly, smiling at the excitement around her. Margaret was going to be a wonderful mother-in-law. She had brought the bouquet of flowers Jennifer would carry. The children were in and out of the room. Both Tiffany and Amy were going to carry flowers down the aisle, and all of the boys, Greg, Tom and Alexander were recruited to help Scott. Jennifer knew at the reception she would be meeting much of Scott's extended family, and she took a deep breath as she left the dressing room, escorted by Rachel and Beth. "They are seating the family," Peter told her as she joined him at the top of the stairs. He smiled at his wife. "Two minutes," he told them. "Are you nervous?" he asked, offering Jennifer his arm. He was going to give her away.

"I'll be fine once I'm down the aisle," she replied. "The church is full?"

Peter smiled. "Yes. Scott looks calm on the outside, but it's covering one very nervous guy. He was pacing earlier, when he thought he was alone."

The doors to the auditorium were opened, and the music began. It was time. The girls went first, followed by the bridesmaids, then Peter squeezed her hand and Jennifer was walking into the church on the arm of her brother. The flowers in the church were overflowing with color and fragrance, Heather had outdone herself. She could see Scott standing at the front of the church with Brad at his side. He looked so dignified: tall, strong and confident. As she caught his gaze he smiled, and she saw him start to relax. She smiled back.

When she reached the front of the aisle, Scott took her hand in his, and Jennifer relaxed, finally, where she felt safe and protected. His grip was firm and strong and confident.

She listened to the service, and when the time came to exchange vows, she placed both of her hands in Scott's and faced him, enough love for a lifetime shining in her eyes.

"Jennifer St. James, do you take Scott Williams to be your lawfully wedded husband, to love, honor and cherish, for richer or poorer, in sickness and in health, till death do you part?"

"I do," she answered, smiling at the man who was to be her husband.

"And do you, Scott Williams, take Jennifer St. James to be your lawfully wedded wife, to love, honor and cherish, for richer or poorer, in sickness and in health, till death do you part?"

"I do," Scott replied with conviction, smiling at Jennifer. She gently squeezed his hands.

Brad handed Scott Jennifer's wedding ring, and he smiled and kissed the back of her hand before sliding it on her finger. Jennifer accepted his from Rachel. Her hands trembled as she slipped it on his finger, annoying her, but making him smile and softly whisper, "I love you," as they turned to face the front of the church again. She looked up at him and grinned. "Did Peter tell you I almost fainted at my first wedding?" she whispered.

"Now you tell me," Scott replied in a whisper, amused. "No wonder he said Brad had smelling salts in his pocket. I thought they were for me." He still held her hand, determined not to release it again, now that the service was almost over. They lit the large candle on the table, shared communion, then Rachel was handing Jennifer back her bouquet, and the minister was turning to the congregation. "Ladies and gentleman, may I present Mr. and Mrs. Williams," the minister said with a smile. "Scott, you may kiss your bride."

Scott took his time, amusing Jennifer, who stood patiently as he smoothed back her short veil, linked his left hand with hers, gently tipped her chin up with his right hand and lowered his head to share their first kiss as husband and wife. He was smiling, a deeply satisfied smile, and it made her smile in return.

They walked down the aisle holding hands, Jennifer very content to leave the details now to Scott.

* * *

"Doing okay?" Scott leaned over to ask, taking advantage of a slight break in the guests coming through the reception line.

"Yes," Jennifer told her husband, loving the word *husband*. "My hand's taking a beating with all the handshakes, but I'll make it."

"Pain?"

He would get her out of the line if she so much as hinted at pain. Jennifer could tolerate it. "No, just annoyingly stiff."

"Does that mean your pool game might be a little off?" he asked with a grin.

"Don't count on it," she replied.

Jennifer enjoyed the reception, mingling with Scott's family, her husband never far from her side. He was a dashing figure in his tux, and she loved watching him. It seemed to be mutual, because he had her blushing more than she could remember doing in recent months. Everyone wanted to ask about the fire, and she found herself trying to keep the details to a minimum. Heather, who now considered Jen second only to an angel, gave her a happy Mary Elizabeth to flirt with for the pictures everyone requested.

Scott maneuvered her to the back of the reception hall. "Let's slip away and get changed. If it fits, wear the outfit I had Rachel put in the dressing room for you. I'll meet you in the lobby."

"We'll miss the rice."

"Not with Tiffany and Greg around, but I figure it's worth a shot," he replied with a chuckle, kissing her at the top of the stairs where they needed to part company. "Hurry."

Rachel helped Jennifer slip carefully out of her wedding dress, and they both laughed when they saw the gift from Scott. He had sent jeans, socks with wedding bells on them, new tennis shoes. It was the sweatshirt that brought the laughter. It was white with a beautiful red heart with Scott Loves Jennifer written on the front and Jennifer Loves Scott written on the back, all the kids' initials at the bottom as the designers.

Jennifer met Scott at the top of the stairs. He had changed into jeans and a company sweatshirt. He grinned and gave her a hug. "Thanks for wearing it."

"Are you kidding? I love it."

"Brad has brought the car around, it's been appropriately decorated, though I was able to talk the kids out of tin cans attached to the bumper. We've got friends standing two-deep in line to toss rice."

"You're loving this."

He grinned. "Of course. Now that all the ceremony is over, it's time to have fun."

She laughed and let him tug her to the door. "Ready to run?" he asked.

As they came through the doorway, the rice began to fly amidst laughter from their family and friends. They hurried to the car through the shower of rice. Scott came around to open Jennifer's door, get her safely seated. She had to bat a few balloons from inside the car before she could get in. Scott circled the car, grinning at the Just Married wording on the windows. Brad handed him the car keys. "The car is filled up, sodas are in the cooler, and I made sure all your luggage is still there."

"Thanks, friend," Scott said with a grin.

Scott found his sunglasses and slipped them on, looked over at his new wife and grinned. "Ready to go?"

She laughed as she tried to get the rice out of her hair. "Please."

She watched where they were going until she saw Scott

turn onto the interstate. She settled back in her seat and made herself comfortable. The stress was over, and she was now conserving her energy for the evening. It had been a very long day already. She closed her eyes with a sigh.

"You were beautiful today."

She turned her head on the seat and smiled. "You looked dashing in your tux."

"You think so?"

"Most definitely. Can you tell me where we are going?"

"I thought we could use a little uninterrupted time. We are borrowing the home of friends for the next week. It's a country place, secluded. There's a pool table in the den, so we can play a few friendly games. There are horses to ride and cross-country trails to ski if we get some snow. I also thought you might enjoy the peace and quiet to work on your book. Rachel transferred everything to my laptop, and your notes are in the briefcase."

She reached over and hugged him. "Thank you."

"You're welcome." He gestured to the map on the seat beside him. "It's a four-hour drive, so it's going to be late when we arrive. Why don't you try to get comfortable and catch a nap? There should be a couple of pillows in the back seat, complements of Trish."

Jennifer found them. "Thank you, Trish." She piled them up against the door and made herself comfortable.

Scott looked over, a short time later, to find Jennifer had fallen asleep. Her hands were slack in her lap, her breathing low and level, and her head was leaning against the locked side door, the seat belt holding her still. He smiled. His wife.

Thank you, Lord. I owe you one.

Her eyes had been so crystal clear since the day she had come awake. No fear, no tension, no stress. It was the Jennifer he had seen in pictures from years ago. She hadn't told him why the fear was gone, and he didn't intend to press. She'd tell him when she was ready.

It was a glorious sunset an hour later, wonderful in color. Scott considered waking up Jennifer to enjoy the view but decided against it. She was sleeping so peacefully. She woke about twenty minutes before they arrived, stretched her arms and settled back, relaxed.

It was a beautiful home. Scott led Jennifer to the front door and, with a smile, carried her over the threshold.

Scott found Jennifer in the kitchen when he came downstairs from carrying in the luggage. "They left a nice note," Jennifer said, gesturing to the counter. "They also left dinner. There's Italian beef and a wonderful cheese dip, all the fixings for salad. Interested?"

"Very. I don't remember lunch."

Jennifer smiled. "See if you can find the plates, and I'll get started on the salad."

They played four games of pool after dinner, effectively dispelling any notion of her stiff hand having affected her game. After soundly beating her husband for the fourth time, Jennifer couldn't prevent a giggle as he swept down on her after she sank the eight ball and picked her up off the floor. "You are lethal at this game. I think it's time we did something else."

She wrapped her arms around his neck. "What did you have in mind?"

He nibbled along her jaw before finding her mouth. "Let's go to bed." His husky request got a blush, an intimate smile and a nod. "I like that idea." She thought about the gifts and whether to mention them but decided against it when her hand found its way inside his shirt as he carried her toward the steps. The agenda for the night was not going to need help. She let her hand play across his chest as he reached the first landing and watched his eyes turn dark with passion. She smiled and slid her hand lower. "Jen, I need thirty seconds of good behavior here, or you're going to get dropped on your tush," he warned. She chuckled and kissed his jaw. She had missed being married.

"Which side of the bed do you prefer?" he asked as he carried her into the guest bedroom.

"Yours," she replied with a smile.

He claimed a kiss as he very gently lowered her to the bed. "I love you," he whispered.

She wrapped her arms around his neck. "I love you more," she said with a smile.

He was laughing as she tugged him down.

It was sometime before dawn when Jennifer awoke, tucked beside Scott, held safe and secure by his arms, her head resting against his shoulder. She moved to restore circulation in her left hand and felt his arms tighten.

"Hey, you're awake," he whispered drowsily, awakened by her movements.

She kissed his jaw. "Told you I liked your side of the bed," she murmured.

Even half-asleep, he smiled at her comment. "You can have it every night. I like sleeping with you," he replied, enjoying immensely waking up with a wife instead of alone. She chuckled at where his hands moved and leaned over to kiss him. "It's mutual."

Epilogue

"**D**o you think something might have happened? He's late."

"Twenty minutes," Scott replied, folding his arms around Jennifer's shoulders as she stood watching out the front window.

"His first night on his own with the car. Are you sure he was ready for this?"

Scott smiled. "He'll be fine. And there will be a good reason he's late. He's been a model of good behavior since we put the possibility of a car before him. He's not going to lose the privilege he's worked months to achieve by doing something stupid the first time he gets the keys. Let's wait and see what he says."

"Well, I worry about him."

"Of course you do, you're his mom," Scott replied, leaning over to kiss her.

She leaned back, letting him take her weight. "How are our other two? Asleep?"

"Hopefully," Scott replied, having been the one to get soaked giving the twins their bath. Not that he minded. The three-year-olds both looked like their mom and they loved to flirt. "Kay wanted Quigley to sleep in their room and April practically pleaded with me to say yes, so I let the shaggy beast have the rug."

Jennifer grinned. "What did April do, flutter her eyelashes at you?"

Scott smiled. "She likes to think it makes a difference, and who am I to dissuade her? April is easier to resist than Kay. Kay has that Daddy smile." He slid his hands around to link with hers. "Come on, it's not the in thing for parents to stand at the window and watch for their kids. You have to do it with some class. Like sit on the couch." Jennifer reluctantly let herself be pulled away from the window. Their adopted son, Paul, had just got his license, and it was tough to let go, accept the fact he was growing up, would turn seventeen in a few weeks. After five years, the first two of which had been marked by incredible battles of will, their son was now pushing straight A's in school, lettering in track and able to wipe the table with both of them at pool. She loved him with a passion. Add Kay and April who formed Paul's personal adoring fan club, and Scott who thought his son should be a fighter jock or president, and Paul had the deck firmly stacked in his favor.

"It's a chaperoned date, you don't have to worry about him. Kevin won't let him get into any trouble," Scott reminded her.

Jennifer smiled as she leaned her head back against Scott's arm. "I know. Kevin has turned into a great youth minister."

He stole a kiss. "Are we ready for Morgan?" Their lawyer was coming out in the morning to discuss a fourteen-year-old runaway who desperately needed a home.

"I think so. Are you sure we're ready to do this again?"

"I think it's the mission God dropped in our laps," Scott replied seriously. "I love being a dad. You're not having any reservations, are you?"

Jennifer shook her head. "No."

The lights of a car came through the living room window. "Thirty minutes. Not too bad," Scott commented, glancing at his watch.

Paul swooped in the front door, dropping his jacket across the banister. "You know, one of these days I'm going to catch you two more than just smooching on that couch," he remarked, dropping into the leather chair across from them with a grin. "I'm in love," he said dramatically.

"Really?" Jennifer asked, sitting up. He and Tiffany had been spending a lot of time together, and tonight wasn't their first date.

He rolled his eyes. "No...the car. Even Kevin says it's cool." Praise from his idol. "Tiff's not too bad, either," he told his mom, amused at her look. "I was late because Kevin had to pop the hood of the car and take a look. Oh, and he wants me to be the junior high social director this summer. I told him I would ask you."

Scott grinned. "Do you want to?"

"Me? Have lots of munchkins around looking up to me and hanging on every word I say? Now who would like that?" he replied, grinning.

"You," Scott replied. He glanced at Jennifer. "Sure, it's fine with us. You might want to ask Tiffany if she'd like to help out."

"I kind of planned on doing that," Paul replied with a grin.

Jennifer settled herself into the crook of Scott's arm with a smile. She loved being a mom.

* * * * *

Dear Reader,

Thank you for reading *The Marriage Wish*. It holds a special place in my heart as my first book published. As a preemie myself, I've often thought about what would have happened had I not lived. This story was born while looking through the baby photo albums my mother kept through my long hospital stay.

I would love to hear from you. You can find me online at: www.deehenderson.com, e-mail: dee@deehenderson.com or write me c/o Steeple Hill, 233 Broadway, Ste. 1001, New York, NY 10279.

Sincerely,

Dee Henderson